When we've said goo

Telepathy-

From the Ancient Greek, *tele* meaning "distant" and *pathos* or *–patheia* meaning

"feeling, perception, passion, affliction or experience".

Scientists do not view telepathy as "real".

For my son, Daniel -

"In whom I am well pleased"

.

To Viktoria

Paul

Part One. When we've said Goodbye.

Chapter One.

The courier knew where the house was; he had been there many times over the past two years. As he swung his lime green van onto the recently concreted farm track, he could see the renovated stone cottage off to his right and the man to whom he was delivering, sat on a dirty white plastic bench. The man stood and walked towards the courier and opened the rusted metal five bar gate to let him drive through. Christian noted that the man leaned heavily on the walnut hiking stick he still favoured. The man could be any age between forty and sixty and was at the top end of that scale. His rough hewn face showed no feelings, the eyes deep set and devoid of expression.

"Morning Christian" the man spoke, smiling a smile that failed to reach the eyes. Christian leapt from his van and handed over a slim brown cardboard wrapped package, Amazon emblazoned across it.

"Sign here, boss" Christian said and waited while the man scrawled his signature on the screen of the hand held device.

"I hope that's what you've been waiting for" Christian said. His customer nodded and walked away slowly, as if in a trance, staring at the package held lovingly in his calloused hands. Christian reversed the van and drove away not looking back because he knew the customer was not watching.

The man was Lee, father, writer, and armed forces veteran, in that order. The package contained the first copy of his first ever book published under his own name, "When we've said goodbye". Two years of writing, editing, changing and revising had seemed like a lifetime but it was all over now. The fruits of his efforts were there, resting in the palm of his hand. He felt proud but also apprehensive. His first book was published under a pseudonym, mainly because of it's sensitive writing about Northern Ireland and Lee's part in the 'Troubles'.

'At long last!' he sighed, gazing at the front cover that featured a black and white photo of a girl, blonde with one eyebrow pierced, who seemed to be deep in thought, cigarette smoke drifting across the picture. A photo taken by a young lady in Serbia and sent to Lee especially for his book cover. The print was in gold on a grey background giving the book an expensive yet haunting look. The book, a tragic-novel, was a labour of love but had, at times, felt like a punishment. As a love story, Lee was probably the least equipped to write it. He had known true love only once, it had lasted only six years and he was still bitter. A friend had suggested he write a story of love as a way to purge his heart of hatred. Lee would be the first to admit that it had not worked. He knew it would cause a stir if not a storm among people from his past but did not care. Lee had several hours before his son, Jack, returned home from school and so he poured himself a congratulatory glass of Retsina, and sat in the sunshine and opened his book. Once more, he gazed at the stone walls of the cottage, which was over one hundred years old and smiled. Even with double-glazing, the place looked what it was, old but sturdy. The countryside around Lee was quiet, the campsite all but empty and even the birds had stopped singing, or maybe Lee simply failed to hear them. As the cotton wool like clouds cleared away, the sun shone down on Lee and, as the day grew warmer, even though he knew every word by heart, he started to read.

When we've said goodbye.

"Think of me, think of me fondly."

Chapter One.

July in North Wales. A rare hot summer's day in the valley between Moel Smytho and Moel Eilio, two mountains overlooking the 'Farm amongst the Ash Trees', and the bbq's were out all around. Mostly at the campsite but one in particular in the garden of Ynysoed, a large detached house on the farm, which sat between the two mountains at the edge of Snowdonia. Ian and Andrea had lived in the area for nearly twenty years and loved the summer days when they could invite friends for a meal and a few drinks. The guests included Pav, a single father to thirteen-year-old Andrew. Pav was slim and average height, brown greying hair that he liked to keep short. His face normally bore a smile. There was something about Pav that portrayed strength, leadership and loyalty. A single father with a dubious past, he kept to himself except for his friendship with Ian and Andrea. For some reason, Pav seemed to be at ease with them. Pav had learned the hard way that people in the area he had chosen to live were a back biting bunch, not worthy of attention. The owners of the campsite were an intolerant couple, only interested in making money no matter how. Pav had managed to keep his cool in some trying circumstances with this couple but his patience was wearing thin. He had moved to this area two years ago from the East Midlands, along with Andrew, his boisterous son. Not many people knew why they had chosen this part of Wales to live in, but Ian did. When Pav and Andrew moved to Wales, Pav realised that he needed a companion for when Andrew was at school, and also to occupy Andrew during the holidays. That companion came in the form of a

Border Collie called Pende. Pende was black and white and nearly five years old when Pav and his son saw her and the dog charmed them both instantly. Pende had been abandoned some five miles away and Ian had found her. Knowing that Pav would be the ideal owner, Ian brought the underweight, under nourished and very frightened dog to Pav. Andrew and the dog were inseparable and Pav and Pende would often be seen tramping the hills together, Pende bounding ahead but returning the instant she heard her master whistle. The dog kept clear of the sheep on the farm but could have been a sheepdog if given the chance. She slept at the foot of Andrew's bed during the night and by Pav's feet during the day. Pav knew that Pende would miss him when the time came and so gave the animal all the attention and love he could spare.

Over the two years they had been friends, Ian and Pav had often worked and socialised together and enjoyed each other's company. Many were the time they would just sit by a fire, no words spoken, just 'living' the dream. Ian would say that Pav had been somewhat distant in the past few weeks. Maybe because he had been able to send Andrew on a long holiday to Australia that friends had invited the boy on. Pav was a writer. His written works were in an area that no one locally had any need to look at. He specialised in articles about children with Special Education Needs but had had success with three books. Pav said they were fiction but no one was sure. The food was cooking nicely and the beer was in full flow and Ian glanced across at Pav, seeing him reclining in the deck chair, looking relaxed, maybe even asleep.

"Hey, Pav," he called, "Your turn on the fire, mate".

Pav did not stir.

'Bloody typical', Ian thought, 'He's having a kip.'

Ian adjusted the blue and white striped apron his wife had bought him and walked the few yards to where Pav was seated and shook his shoulder. Pav jerked and floundered around, spitting and foaming at the mouth, his eyes rolling wildly. His back arched and his eyes bulged but not a sound did he make. Ian's first thought was that Pav had had too much to drink but seeing his friend behaving this way sounded alarms in his head. Quickly, he grabbed Pav and laid him on the floor in the recovery position.

"Call an ambulance!" Ian yelled to his wife. "Pav's having some sort of seizure!"

Considering they lived in the middle of the countryside, the ambulance took only eight minutes to arrive and the paramedics soon took over. Assessing the situation, they told Ian,

"Ysbyty Gwynedd in about thirty minutes. Are you following?"

Ian nodded and he and Andrea jumped into their Toyota and took off after the ambulance with its blue lights flashing and sirens wailing, to the hospital. When they arrived, Pav was taken into A+E and Ian and Andrea watched the gurney being rushed through swing back doors, away from the reception. When the news came, it was a bolt straight out of the blue. The Doctor, a young looking South African man with freckles and a beard just about growing, approached them.

"Are you relatives?" he asked.

"Friends," Ian replied. "His son is on holiday in Australia."

"Get him back, ASAP," the doctor said. "He doesn't have long, maybe a few days."

"Why?" asked Ian. "For Gods sake, it was just a barbeque. He didn't have much to drink, honest. And a few days for what?"

The doctor looked harassed.

"His tumour has grown too big." He said. "The pressure on the brain is at its peak."

Andrea gasped.

"Tumour? What tumour?"

"I thought you were his friends?" the doctor said. "Pav is a regular here at the moment. He has a brain tumour that is malignant. He cannot, repeat, cannot be saved. He has been on medication but there is no sign that he has taken any recently. He was given the option of chemotherapy a few months ago but declined. At the moment, he is at peace. The coma may well help him from this world to the next without too much pain. A thought. Has he actually *told* his son?"

Ian and Andrea looked at each other. Their non-reply spoke volumes.

"In that case, may I suggest you telephone anyone who he loves and inform them and I mean anyone. At this moment in time anybody who can make his, erm, transition, easier, would be most welcome here."

Ian and Andrea left the hospital in a daze. Once in the car and after several moments, Ian turned to Andrea.

"You know who I have to call, don't you?" he asked.

After over twenty years together, they were still on the same wavelength and Andrea replied,

"Yes. Ffion. But Ian, how the hell can you do that? What if she doesn't want to know? If that's the case, how could you possibly tell Pav if he wakes up?"

Ian could not provide the answer to that question. That was a matter to be decided if, and when, it arose.

Pav

Pav, he had a surname but rarely used it, not since his time in the British Army. Pav had attended a boarding school and, at the age of fifteen, had realised where his future lay, as a soldier. When he mentioned this to his Careers Advisor, the man had simply laughed. He believed that Pav, at a mere five feet six inches tall and slim built, was not soldier material. Pav disagreed and started looking at what the Army was up to, what it could offer him and what he could offer the army. The year was 1969 and the 'Troubles' had kicked off in Northern Ireland. Pav read every news report, listened to the radio and watched the television so that he could get as much information as possible. He also read as many history books about the troubled province as the school library held. If he had been asked at that time, Pav would have said that his sympathies lay with the Catholic population in that they had the worst housing and the lowest paid jobs. When the Civil Rights Movement took action to put matters right, they were beaten and, in some cases, shot. The Catholics were the underdogs in a modern society. At least, that is how Pav saw it. Deep down, the studious young schoolboy felt that he could do some good by becoming a soldier and volunteering to serve in Belfast. After leaving school, Pav worked in a Building Society in Coventry, a job that made him bored and frustrated. As soon as he was seventeen, he went off to the Army Careers Information Office and started the process of signing up. However, because he was under eighteen years old, he needed his Mothers signature on the recruiting papers. Pavs Mother initially refused but relented when Pav merely stated that he could, and would, join the following year, without her permission. Pavs brother was already in the Royal Air Force but Pav had no intention of following his footsteps. Pav joined the Royal Corps of Transport and trained in Aldershot. After just three months, he had gained three inches in height and three stone in weight, and had developed a physique. On his first leave his friends hardly recognised the quiet, skinny boy they had grown up with. Pav also developed a confidence, which was not always to his advantage. When he returned to Aldershot, Pav signed up for a parachute course, which he passed with honours. His first 'posting' was to London as a Staff Car driver, chauffeuring Senior Officers about. Pav was popular among all ranks of officer and earned a reputation for skilled driving, reliability and discretion. He was assigned to drive the recently promoted Chief of Staff, London District and, on his first visit to the Brigadiers house, handed the officer his mail. The Brigadier opened the first letter, which blew up, taking his left hand with it. Pav took control of the situation, calling for an ambulance and then the Military Police. For the next three weeks, Pav drove relatives of the Brigadier all over the country, dressed in civilian clothes and armed with a loaded pistol. His hours were long and often arduous but Pav never complained. When the Brigadier left hospital, Pav drove him and his wife to Heathrow Airport and was stunned when the officer told Pav to keep his car for the next two weeks. Pav enjoyed that BMW 2002 to it's fullest. Shortly after returning from holiday, the Brigadier retired and a new officer took his place. Looking back, Pav would say that this was most fortuitous for him. The new Chief of Staff had been the Brigade Commander in Londonderry at the time of Bloody Sunday and Pav listened to his new boss with rapt pleasure. He learned the truth about that fateful Sunday and his resolve to go to Northern Ireland was ever more strengthened.

After six months with his new boss, Pav was offered a chance to go to Northern Ireland as driver to the Brigade Commander in Belfast. He jumped at the chance despite his friends advising him not to. At that time, Pav was dating a young female soldier who said she thought Pav had a 'death wish'. Pav smiled and set off by train to Liverpool and then the overnight ferry to Belfast, full of anticipation.

When the ferry docked next morning, Pav felt let down. He wondered why he could not hear shooting, rioting and bombs. The city seemed normal with the exception of the troops manning vehicle checkpoints and patrolling the streets. Buses ran, people moved around freely and all seemed to be at peace. Pav was directed to a coach with the other soldiers and was amazed when only one lightly armed soldier joined them. In answer to his query, the soldier smiled and said,

"We're in civvies today, no need for an armed escort, it brings too much attention to us."

On arrival at Lisburn, Pav was the only soldier alighting and felt alone for the first time since joining up. That soon changed as he met the Regimental Sergeant Major who got Pav settled in. Once again, Pav became an integral part of Rover Group, the Brigade Commanders crew of drivers and escorts and Pav saw the 'Troubles' at first hand. Shootings, bombings and riots were his staple diet over the next five years. Normally, drivers in his position were changed every two years but, because Pav had an expert knowledge of Belfast and a unique understanding of the situation, he was asked to stay on twice. In that time, Pav married and had a son but, to his shame now, he devoted his life to the army that had given him purpose and a quality of life. He rose to the rank of Sergeant but, at the end of his fifth year, Pav had to make a choice. Sign on for longer or leave. To sign on meant leaving to go to Germany, to leave meant going home to Coventry as a civilian. Pav found a compromise. He would leave the army, stay in Northern Ireland and join the Royal Ulster Constabulary. Ann, his wife, reluctantly agreed to this compromise but told Pav that, if it did not work out, she was going home to Sunderland, her hometown.

Pav left the army but, because he could not join the RUC straight away, had three months to wait. He joined a crisp company and became a van salesman selling crisps all over Belfast. By this time, he had grown a beard and let his hair grow down to his shoulders. He looked just like any other man in Belfast. Selling came naturally to him and he even made sales along the predominantly Catholic Falls Road, using his Belfast accent when necessary. To his knowledge he was never compromised, if he had been he would have been shot on sight. When stopped by checkpoints, he reverted to his English accent and that led the troops to believe that he was undercover. Pav often chuckled at that. Not all his time in Belfast was happy though.

Chapter 1

Silver grey mists, swirling in front of his eyes, much like cigarette smoke under a ceiling fan. No sounds heard, no emotions felt, no pain suffered. Limbo, somewhere between life and death, a strange sensation, neither hot nor cold, neither breathing nor dead. A time without time.

Am I dreaming? What happened to the barbeque? Where the hell am I? I am lying in a hospital bed; harsh bright white light is forcing me back into the mattress. Pinning me down. Why are there soldiers around? I see them, armed to the teeth, facing away from me. Protecting me? From what? Or from who? All is silent in this place of safety. No one moves not even the soldiers. A memory floods my mind and I wonder why it is me who is in hospital, not Les. We had an argument about who was to be 'tail end Charlie' on our patrol. I outranked Les but he wanted his turn at being the last man to form our 'brick' of four. The argument was heated and, in the end, I had backed down. Our patrol was late leaving the base at Springfield Road Police Station and the CO was giving us grief. We 'hard targeted' through the gates of Springfield Road police station and ran flat out for the first three hundred yards. So far so good. Twenty minutes later, we turned off the Falls Road and into Percy Street. A new Security Interface had been built and it was down to us to check it was still in one piece. I went first, Caesar (Norman Hobson) second, Legs (Keith Diamond) third and then Les. Only one streetlight shone and I raced through its ambient glow. Caesar and Legs followed swiftly but Les hung back for a few seconds too long. Then, as if he felt he had a point to make to me, he ambled through the glow of the lamp and a shot rang out. Les went down as if pole axed, which I suppose he was. Legs and I opened fire in the only direction a shot could have come from, peppering a brick wall fifty yards away until our mags were empty. Then Caesar emptied his twenty rounds in the same direction while I dragged Les into cover behind a builders skip. Legs called 'contact' over the radio and we took up defensives, waiting for the Saracen Ambulance to reach us. Silence fell until, five minutes later, we heard the scream of gears as the Saracen driver roared into the street. We all piled in, lifting Les carefully but the medic told us it was too late. Les had gone.

One shot through the head. One-shot Willie had struck again. Because I lost a verbal argument with him. Les was dead because of me. Was that why I was in the hospital? I glance to my left. Les is there. He should have been a film star, not a Military Policeman. Dark hair, almost cherubic face, physique that Arnie would have died for. He looked at me, eyes closed, face pale. I heard him say, 'it wasn't your fault, Pav' Yet it was and I will never, ever forgive myself for what happened. It should have been me! The soldiers disappear and doctors in their pristine white coats take their place. They look down at me, faces sombre. Have I died? Their lips move but I hear no sound. I cannot move. My sight swivels left but my eyes are closed. Les has gone too. Maybe now would be a good time to panic?

Pav stirred restlessly in the hospital bed. The nurse stared at the monitors and noted the heightened brain activity. Spikes showed that Pavs brain was capable of something, however the nurse could not tell what. 'Maybe there's hope after all,' she thought. The brain signals gradually slowed until hardly any movement showed on the screen.

*

Three days later.

Ian paced the living room, cordless phone in his left hand, waiting, trying to decide if he should even make the call. He had no idea what the reception would be, that's if someone even answered. The number was a landline number and he suspected it might even be discontinued now. Ian and Pav were neighbours and Pav appreciated Ian's intelligence, ready wit and sense of humour. In many ways they were both alike. 'Right' he thought, 'it's now or never.' And he dialled carefully. Having waited three days before making this move, Ian wanted to get it over and done with, no matter the outcome.

The phone rang for almost a minute before it was answered. A grunt, similar to what Neanderthal Man might have sounded like.

"Unghh?". Ian took a deep breath and composed his thoughts.

"Can I speak to Ffion Stone, please?"

"S'callin?" was the response. Ian had heard about Damien, Ffion's teenage son but nothing prepared him for the arrogance and ignorance the reply portrayed.

"She doesn't know me, my name is Ian and I need to talk to her about someone she used to know."

There was no response to that, just the sound of the phone being dropped, or thrown, onto the floor. Heavy footsteps sounded, like bare feet slapping on parquet flooring, and then there was silence.

Eventually, the phone was picked up and a soft, rather cultured female voice said, "Can I help you?"

"My name is Ian and I live in North Wales. I am a friend of Pav". He let that sink in before continuing. When no response was forthcoming, he continued "Pav is seriously ill in hospital. At the moment he is in a coma. It's a brain tumour and he doesn't have long to live. He doesn't know I am calling you. I got your number from his mobile, under 'In Case of Emergency'. Ian stopped, thinking he had blurted it out, not explained the reason for his call.

Fi paused before replying. Visions of her life with Pav flashing across her thoughts.

"And you are calling me, why?" she said, her tone now cold, aloof and decidedly unfriendly.

"Look, Ms Stone, Pav has told me enough about your relationship, how he fouled it up and so on. It's just that, now he is so close to death, I thought you ought to know. He and I have been friends for two years now and I want to see him sent off properly."

Ffion replied immediately, "Again, what does he want from me? Pav has two ex wives, maybe you should be calling them"

"Pav wants nothing from you that I know of. He's dying, in a coma and has only a few days to stay alive. You were the only woman he really, really loved and I hoped you could find it in your heart to come and say goodbye to him."

Ian waited. He thought he heard a sniff and the sound of a nose being blown. Seconds stretched and the silence was almost deafening. Eventually she spoke, her tone soft and, almost, concerned.

"Would he even understand that I was there?"

Ian started to feel relaxed.

"The Consultant thinks that he knows but can't communicate with us. If you saw him you would see why."

Ffion paused before replying.

"It's a long way to drive, two hundred miles. I'm not sure I can do it."

"If I know Pav, Ffion, he would *walk* two hundred miles to see you if *you* needed *him*!" Ian said, impatience sounding sharply in his voice. If he was honest, Ian thought he was wasting his time on the call but he had to try. His wife, Andrea, had thought the call was a mistake but Ian just wanted to help his friend. During his many chats with Pav one thing was clear. Pav wanted just one chance to see Ffion again before he died. He obviously had something to say to her, maybe an apology or to beg forgiveness, who knows.

Ffion spoke angrily to Ian "If you know Pav so well, you will know about the betrayal!"

Ian thought for a second before replying, "That's none of my business Ffion. All I'm trying to do is make Pavs last wish come true."

Ffion thought for a few moments. What did she have to lose? Come to that, what did she have to gain? Lucky this happened during the school summer holidays, if it had been term time, well, she obviously could not have taken the time off for, for what? To go and see someone two hundred miles away, someone who would not survive the week let alone the year. Someone who had once loved her very dearly. Someone who had betrayed her in the worst possible way. Someone she had grown to hate with a tremendous passion? Her family would not approve, not by a long way. Did she owe Pav this? Did she owe him anything at all? Three years, no contact between them, and now, some man rings out of the blue with this sob story. Ffion stared around the living room. All browns and beiges, inset lights casting an almost romantic glow, the oatmeal shag carpet beneath her bare feet feeling soft and reassuring. The room where she and Pav used to cuddle up on the sofa to watch television, late into the night. Then her glance stopped. She stared at the real oak unit against the far wall and, more poignantly, at the top shelf. On it was placed, in prominent view, the now dusty music box. Not a box as such, it was a figurine of a boat with the Phantom of the Opera taking Christine to his lair. Pav had bought it for her five years ago. He had had it sent from America and Ffion was touched by his ingenuity. If she turned the key underneath, she would hear Michael Crawford sing 'The Music of the Night' from the show they had both seen and loved so much. Ffion had not turned that key for over three years and she did so now, letting the music close in around her mind. Ian waited patiently, hearing the song in the background but not knowing its significance.

When the song ended, Ffion sighed. "Where is he?" she asked. Ian gave her the address of the hospital and the ward name.

"He's in a private Intensive Care Unit."

"I'm not promising anything, I need to think about things." Ffion said.

"That's fine," replied Ian, "Just do me a favour, call me to let me know if you are on your way, will you?"

Ffion agreed and said "How long does he have?"

"Forty eight hours at the most. He's weak but putting up a good fight. The tumour is growing rapidly now. Pavs tumour is classed as a Grade IV, a high-grade tumour. The doctors may have been able to cut some of it away but that would not have cured him. Pav knew the score, decided against the biopsy. He was told two months ago, was offered chemotherapy but refused. Never told me, the bastard! It was only when he collapsed at our house that we found out. He's been in a coma since, three days."

Ian's voice started to break; he took a deep breath and continued, "He spoke about you all the time. Never a bad word. Keeps your photo on his mobile, often showed it to my wife and me. He would often sit on his decking, laptop beside him, looking through all the pictures he has of you. Hundreds of them! I think I know them by heart now too. Sad really. He has hardly slept these past two years but recently, not at all. I would often see him in the middle of the night, sitting on his decking, smoking. It's as if, well, as if he did not want to miss anything. Now I know why"

Ffion thought for a moment before asking "Why did he move to Wales?"

Ian responded straight away, not needing to think his answer through,

"Distance, Ffion. He couldn't bear to live so close to you. Knowing that he might see you at any time caused him incredible pain. He believed it was better that neither of you had any more heartache. Here, he believed he could lose himself and repair the heart that was so badly broken. I don't think it worked."

Inside, Ian was thinking 'why the hell do you *think* he moved two hundred miles away from you' but he kept his thoughts to himself, for the time being at least.

Ffion queried, "What took you three days to telephone me?"

Ian sighed deeply and paused before answering the question he had most dreaded, "To be honest, we didn't think you would be interested. My wife and I discussed this and eventually decided to give you the chance to do right by Pav, maybe to make amends. Is that so difficult?"

Hearing sobs, Ian realised that Ffion was crying.

"I'm sorry, " he said. "I didn't mean to upset you. Think about it. Please".

Ian put the phone down and cradled his glass of whiskey. 'Jesus,' he thought, 'I never want to have to do anything like *that* again'.

Andrea was sitting at his side, next to a roaring log fire that lit the room with dancing streaks of light. Outside, the darkness folded itself around the mountains, as if mourning Pav.

"I take it that was difficult?" she said. "And what was that music in the background?"

"I've no idea" Ian replied, "It sounded quite sad. Whatever it was, maybe it helped her make the decision. We'll see."

Chapter 2.

Ffion placed the phone on its black and chrome cradle and sat on the blue leather sofa and cried. She actually did not understand why she was crying. Sorrow that her ex partner was dying? Sorrow that it was she who had broken his heart, in revenge? Or was she sad that Ian had even telephoned her and told her the news? Damien slouched into the living room, a can of lager in his hand. His mind was on the Xbox game he had just bought and he was impatient to play it. With his mother in the room, that would be difficult. As usual, he was wearing only boxer shorts, his normal slovenly self. At six feet two, he was the tallest member of the family; even his father was four inches shorter than him. His long spindly legs seemed out of proportion to the rest of his body. A good-looking lad, he made up in looks what he lacked in personality. One ex girlfriend had nicknamed him Bungalow, as she had said, 'there's nothing up top'. Seeing his mother crying he reluctantly muttered

"'S'matter Mum?" he mumbled.

Not that he *cared*; he just hoped that it was nothing serious, like she'd dropped a bottle of wine or something. Ffion dabbed her eyes.

"It's Pav. He's dying."

"Good riddance!" Damien spat. "Better off without him." Although it came out, "beta off wivart 'im". Leicester speak.

Ffion's face turned dark with anger and she glared at her son. He remained quiet as she stumbled into the kitchen and opened the fridge. Tonight's three bottles of wine were chilling nicely. Bundling them into her oversized brown canvas handbag, she turned to Damien and snapped, "I'm going out. OK?"

Damien stepped back. His mother had never raised her voice to him in all his eighteen years. The last time he had not known where she was going had been a nightmare. He had gone to Linda's house and she had called Pav. Damien was sure that the ex soldier, ex boyfriend, had hurt his mum and Damien wanted his dinner! It turned out she had been having sex with some bloke she had met and used when her needs took control. Ffion walked past him, ignoring her German Shepherd and fled through the front door. She did not have far to go. Two semi-detached houses away lived her best friend, Linda. Ffion hammered on the front door tears streaming down her face. Linda opened it and exclaimed "Blimey Fi, what the hell has happened?" Ffion fell into the house and explained all, punctuated by glasses of wine, and sobs.

*

The Intensive Care Unit was plainly decorated and sparsely furnished. A bed, a side table and machines galore. No pictures, just plain off-white walls. The bright lights were oppressive to a visitor, God knew what it did to patients.

'Magnolia must be the in colour,' Ian thought as he sat by the hospital bed. Pav was wired up to drips and monitors, the only sounds in the room being bleeps from machines and a soft whirring of the air conditioning. An oxygen mask covered his mouth and Ian could not see any sign that his friend was actually breathing. Strangely, there was a bottle of orange juice on the bedside table and so Ian helped himself.

"Mate, you look terrible" Ian joked. "Even worse than normal!" No response. Ian leaned closer, almost as if he wanted no one else to hear what he had to say.

"I don't know if you can hear me" he said "but I've spoken to Ffion. She's thinking of coming up to see you. It's a long way though and, well, maybe she's not used to motorway driving. I don't want to build your hopes up, just in case, well, you know."

Was it his imagination or did Pavs finger just twitch? Ian studied the hand but the movement didn't happen again. Ian sighed. He spoke to the Consultant.

"What's that in his right fist?"

The doctor struggled to reply. "We don't know. It looks like a piece of blue paper. We tried to get it out but Pav's grip is solid. Like a vice. Not bad for a man in his weak condition."

Ian laughed, "It's probably his last twenty pound note. He always said if he couldn't take it with him, he wasn't going!"

I heard what Ian said but didn't believe it. Ffion? Coming to see me? Why? To apologise? I doubted it. Maybe to gloat? That was more likely. I could not move, not even to open my eyes but I could still hear and, strangely, I could still see. The doctors talked in hushed tones, in case I caught what they said. For three days I had lain in this hard, poor excuse for a bed. Just the sort of bed a dying person like me deserves. Hard, uncomfortable, unforgiving. The sort of bed that would make you glad to die just to be free of it. Maybe I should have married it! Three days, a lot of time to think, to remember and to regret. But then, I've done a lot of regretting in my life. There is always something you regret more than anything else. Mine was losing Ffion. I loved her so much, it hurt. When the headaches started, five years ago now, she and her friends thought I was exaggerating. Maybe now she knew the truth. I thought the headaches were stress but could not think of anything that stressed me. Except perhaps Ffion. I wish I could speak to her, tell her how much I still love her.

*

Chapter 3.

Three months earlier.

Experience had taught Pav not to believe in coincidences. So therefore, it could not be a coincidence that he was here, at a doctor's surgery, asking for the second MRI scan in four years. Nor could it be a coincidence that the very charming receptionist was called Ffion. And a pretty blonde too! Fate maybe? Pav hoped not. As Pav waited, his doctor, a typical Welsh, hill walking type, dressed in outdoor cord trousers, flannel shirt and green heavy duty body warmer, smiled indulgently and perused the computerised notes carefully.

"Hm, I see you had an MRI in Leicester some time ago. The results indicate a large contusion to the left side of your brain. Nothing to worry about, it says here. Are you still taking the Sumatryptan tablets?" he said.

"Yes" Pav replied, "But they are for Migraine and I don't have a bloody Migraine! I have a mega brain ache, I am sick all the time and sometimes unsteady on my feet. It's embarrassing, people think I'm drunk for goodness sake!"

The doctor paused, "I could increase the dosage if that would help?"

"Tell you what," Pav retorted, "Just give me sleeping tablets or, better still, heavy doses of morphine!"

Doctor Lloyd stroked his ginger goatee thoughtfully and studied his patient.

Pavs headache chose that moment to return and Pav clutched his temples as the pain tore through his head, almost rattling his brain. He winced and his sight was blurred for a few minutes. Eventually, Pav sagged back in the chair, eyes looking at the ceiling, almost at peace. As the pain receded, the doctor watched his patient.

"I'll get that MRI appointment for you. When can you attend?"

"Anytime you like, but make it soon. Please." Pav felt exhausted, as he did every time he had an episode like this. Keeping the headaches secret from his son was even more exhausting than the actual pain itself. As he sat there, Pav thought about his past, or at least, some of the worse parts. Images of bodies flashed through his mind. Some he had killed, some had died at the hands of others. Pav sighed and closed his mind to the past. It had haunted him for too long.

Doctor Lloyd left the room and made a quick call. He was concerned and wanted Pav seen by a specialist as soon as possible. This would call in a big favour and he would owe the Neurologist one in return. And the Professor would be sure to call it in. Ten minutes later he was back.

"Ysbyty Gwynedd, in one hour. Can you get there?"

"Bloody hell, Doc, I know I said soon but that's great. Yes, I'll be there."

Nodding to the receptionist, Pav left the surgery. Now, hopefully, he could get to the bottom of the pain and get rid of it. Looking around at the hills that sat at the edge of Snowdonia Pav felt peaceful again. This was why he and Andrew had moved to North Wales. The scenery, the peace and quiet and the way of life. And the fact that it was two hundred miles away from his ex partner. Despite the distance, hardly an hour went by without Pav thinking of her. He climbed into his ageing but still presentable Sports car and set off.

*

An hour later, Pav was lying on a flat bed, dressed only in a gaudy, ill-fitting hospital gown, waiting to be rolled into the scanner. The radiographer was behind a thick glass window, controlling the speed of the bed into the magnetic field. Occasionally, Pav heard tapping noises as the scanner coils were being turned on and off. Pav lay perfectly still during the fifteen-minute scan and was relieved when it finished. That was probably the most relaxed he had been in years. He dressed, said thanks to the nurses and left for home. All that was left now was to wait for the results. When he arrived home, Pav decided to have a glass of wine and so sat on the decking, reading his post and smoking a cigarette. Alcohol was something he could easily do without but he sometimes actually *needed* a cigarette to stay calm. Now was one of those times.

*

Chapter 4.

At the precise time Pav was under the MRI Scanner, Ffion was having lunch with one of her work colleagues.

Bev was mid fifties, divorced, and slender with a mop of frizzy greying hair. She was also very attractive. The venue for lunch was a café near the school where they both worked as teachers. The café was always busy for lunches and they had been lucky to get a table. Perhaps being regulars had helped. Their conversation was mostly about school gossip until Bev broached a sensitive subject.

"It's been three years now" she said. She did not have to say what had been three years. Three years ago to the day, Pav had moved out of Ffion's house, his life in ruins, his relationship destroyed by some unseen hand. Ffion had made sure that everyone at school knew she was now single, the day Pav was off the scene. Ffion frowned, looking distant.

"Yes, I had remembered. Three years and not a word since that night when I told him something terrible. I don't even know where he is. It's like he disappeared off the face of the earth."

"You mean about your 'friend with benefits' Fi?" Bev asked, with a cruel smile.

"Yes. My 'friend' as you call him. A mistake, him and telling Pav about him. I just wanted to hurt him, but not as much as I did."

Bev placed her hand on Ffion's hand.

"Look Ffion, it's none of my business but, I have to say, Pav never did me any harm. When I was ill, he drove me all over town, doctors and then hospital. He got me the treatment I *needed*. If not for him, I might not be alive now. He looked after me when my daughter was away, and probably kept me sane. I lied to him about Neil and believe me Fi, I hated doing that! I owe Pav and if I had the chance to help him now, I would damned well take it. He did a lot more for you than for me. He helped me because I *needed* help. He would have helped you because he *loved* you. Probably still does. Look at all the things he did for you, which your family would never have thought of! Your fiftieth birthday party. How many of your family helped Pav organise that? Who would have paid to fly your sister over from Oz? I'll tell you Ffion, none! They didn't want to know to be perfectly honest. I didn't particularly *like* Pav but I did respect him for his utmost devotion to you. *I* never met a man like that. Never. That's the truth. And, as for wanting to hurt him, well, you sure as hell succeeded."

Ffion sat back, shocked at the directness of Bevs' speech. She hadn't thought about the fact that she had actually hurt Pav so much he had decided to move away. There was nothing more to say so they ate in silence and then went back to work, subdued to say the least.

*

Ffion was to be fifty in July. Pav had spent six months arranging a surprise party for her. He had sneaked a look at her address book, telephoned her friends and relatives, gaining more contact numbers. In the end, he had nearly a hundred acceptances and many more who could not make it but would send a message. He did it alone, even though he had told Ffion's family what he was planning, they did not offer any assistance. Pav spoke to Ffion's father and had paid for the flight, which would get Suzie to England from Australia in time to surprise the birthday girl. Pav booked a room for them at an opulent hotel in Leicester, then organised food and a disco. On the day, Pav cleaned and polished his Mercedes and put fresh flowers on the back window ledge. Still none of Ffion's family had even offered help. Pav paid for it all. Pav had told Ffion that he was taking her out for a meal to celebrate. Just the two of them. However, Ffion was suspicious and badgered Pav until he admitted he was organising a 'surprise' party for her. Ffion was amazed and realised she had spoilt the element of surprise and begged Pav not to ever tell anyone that she knew about it. He agreed and should have been shocked by Ffions reaction on entering the party room. It was arranged that Damien would keep the guests quiet until Ffion entered the restaurant he had booked and then they would shout 'Surprise!' However, Damien did not keep to the task. Ffion and Pav entered the room and all went silent. Pav resurrected the situation by shouting "Surprise". The two approached the bar and Pav ordered a drink for 'The birthday girl'. What was supposed to happen was that Suzie would stand up with a glass of champagne in her hands and say "Happy birthday Fi". Yet again, Damien failed and Pav had to say, in a loud voice "**A drink for the birthday girl!**" Suzie then appeared from the back of the room and wished her sister a happy birthday. Pav was fuming. He had given Damien a job to do but he had failed, abysmally. Pav suspected it was a deliberate act but said nothing. Ffion did not notice, thank goodness. At the back of her mind was revenge for the betrayal but for that night at least, she would forget it. She and Pav danced together and Ffion smiled for the guests. However, no one took any photos that night. Now, that seems to make sense to Pav but at the time? Pav and Ffion stayed at the hotel and Pav had arranged champagne in the room. When they collapsed into bed at about three in the morning, Ffion was tired, happy, but annoyed. Just what did Pav mean by doing all this? Was he taunting her?

Ffion had no proof other than her suspicions but she firmly believed that Pav had slept with Suzie. Fearing to discuss it with Pav, she had let it fester in her mind, slowly eroding all feelings of love that she had felt for the man.

On the day that Pav had packed his possessions and left Ffion's house, she sat alone in the living room and pondered. Where had her life gone so wrong? Meeting Pav was supposed to be a turning point, a chance for happiness again. Pav was a strange person. An amazing sense of humour and fun, a skilled impressionist and a kind, thoughtful man. But, and it was a big but, Pav could use words to be very aggressive. Many were the time she would make a comment only to be put down in a very acerbic way. He never laid a hand on her though. She slapped him in the face on one occasion but Pav did not respond. Simply shook his head sadly and walked up the stairs to bed. That night, she could not see both sides, just as she had always seen one point, hers.

*

Ffion was gob smacked when, just after seven pm that same day; Pav invited her to his house for a meal. Well, she reasoned, it was Valentines Day. She accepted and drove there. Pav cooked a lovely meal and gave her chocolates and flowers. He had bought them just in case. Ffion enjoyed herself and stayed the night too. If Damien had known eh? But Damien had no idea where his mother was. She had turned her phone off, lest he interrupt. Maybe Pav should have noted the fact that his love was happy to have sex with him but not want him as part of her everyday life? As if she wanted to spread her favours?

*

One week after the scan and Pav was back at the surgery. Was it his imagination or did the receptionist really keep avoiding his eye? Was the sun in the sky just that bit dimmer this morning? Were the birds not singing so loudly today? Just because you're paranoid etc, etc. He sat in the reception and took up an ageing Readers Digest and read about a haunted church in

Cornwall where the vicar was a bit strange to say the least. Pav read that the vicar was so disliked; he put cardboard cutouts of the congregation in the pews because no one came to his church anymore.

'I know how you feel mate' Pav thought.

When his turn came Pav strolled casually into the doctors' room. Doctor Lloyd stood to meet him and that made Pav feel uneasy. Relax, he thought, it's not Belfast for goodness sake! There was another man present, portly, smartly dressed in a three piece navy pin stripe suit and a polka dot bow tie that looked slightly ridiculous on his bulbous neck. The black shirt added to the image of a Mafia Don.

"This is Professor Vaughan Williams. He's a Neurologist at Ysbyty Gwynedd Hospital. He wishes to speak to you."

The Professor sat and explained his area of expertise but Pav hardly heard a word he said. His mind buzzed. 'There's something wrong.' He thought.

Pav stopped the Professor by raising his palm towards the man.

"Just say what it is you have to say. Give it to me straight, no frills, no bullshit!" He said.

The Professor coughed and fidgeted in his seat.

"Alright" he said, "I'll be blunt. Your erm contusion has been masking a large brain tumour. It's malignant, that is to say we cannot operate as it is too well developed. The tumour is classed as a Grade IV, very high. We could perform a biopsy; take a look, maybe cut away some of the tumour. If successful, and that is a very big 'if', we may extend your life by several weeks. The outlook is bleak to put it mildly. There is only so much space the brain can occupy. The growing tumour increases the pressure inside your skull, that's why you have had headaches, sickness and feeling drowsy and lethargic. You may even experience seizures, or fits. Your erm tumour has grown

rapidly recently. Why it has accelerated its speed of growth is a mystery."

Pav had a question to ask; one he thought he already had the answer to.

"Could that explain my bad moods as well?"

The Professor nodded. "Yes. Have you experienced many bad moods? Have you been

violent for example?"

Pav nodded calmly. "Not enough to put anyone in danger." He said, noting the

obvious concern in the medical mans mind.

"How long Doc?" he asked. The Professor was taken aback by the calm directness of

Pavs question.

"If you have Radiotherapy or chemotherapy then maybe up to six months. Without

treatment, two, three at the most. May I suggest you, er, put your house in order?

Contact loved ones etc. We can offer medication that will help numb the symptoms

but I am sorry, that's all we can do. There is one thing you need to remember though.

You may experience a loss of control of your bodily functions"

Pav stared at the man.

"And that means, what?"

The Professor looked Pav in the eyes.

"It means that, quite literally, you will probably vacate your body without any control.

Suddenly, you will know that you need the toilet and it will instantly happen. This

may be a serious side effect of the medication I am going to prescribe for you. I'm

sorry".

"Thank you for your honesty Doc. I have only one loved one and he doesn't need to

share this burden with me. Again, thank you." Pav said and left the room. Outside, he

left his car and walked to the local pub.

'I think I deserve a drink' Pav thought. He set off along the main street, not even seeing people who spoke to him. After a few hundred yards, he came to the local pub. Pav walked into the lounge and downed two vodkas in a hurry. Steve, the barman, looked on, worried because this man normally came in for Cappuccino.

"Everything ok? " he ventured.

"Fine and dandy" Pav replied. "Fine and dandy."

Pav paid and then walked the half-mile home.

'Time to put my house in order' he thought. Pav sat outside on the wooden table and bench set. He stared at the packet of painkillers the doctor had given him. There was no emotion, no sadness, and no grief, at his predicament. Maybe, just maybe, if Pav did not have a wonderful son who needed him, he might be tempted to take the whole packet of tablets and end it all now. But he didn't, couldn't, take that course of action. Pav had always believed that suicide was a coward's way out. Sighing to himself, he made a list of things he needed to do. No way was he having chemo, so time was short. Pav checked his list; it seemed as comprehensive as possible. Then he picked up his mobile phone and made several calls. Some were easier than others. He calmed fears, massaged ego's and bullied officials. By the end of the day, Pav had put all his plans into place, just in time for his son, Andrew, to return home from school.

Chapter 5.

Ffion's tears subsided as the alcohol took effect. It was not unusual for her to down three bottles in one night, but, not so long ago, she had Pav to help her. Not now though. She drank alone at home or on nights out with work colleagues, or with her 'friend with benefits'. Most of her friends and family blamed Pav for her excessive drinking. If only they had known that Ffion had been a heavy drinker long before she met Pav. Ffion turned to Linda,

"Oh my God! Remember the headaches Pav said he had? We thought it was attention seeking! It was true, he *was* ill, even then! That time we took him to hospital; they said it was migraine for God's sake! And I had no sympathy for him. I even said he must have been drinking! And when he stumbled, we thought he had been drinking but he might not have! We laughed so much at him yet all the time it was a medical thing! Oh Linda, what have I done?" She collapsed in tears yet again. Linda put her arm around her friend. "You weren't to know," she said, although her words sounded and felt, hollow. She had liked Pav, thought he was perfect for Ffion. If only she had met someone who had cared about her as much as Pav cared about Ffion. The men Linda met just wanted sex. Not surprising, as she was a very lovely, sexy, blonde lady. Even after three children, she had an hourglass figure and a very pretty face. It was just a shame that Ffion's daughter and youngest son had made life so difficult for him. No wonder he had drank a little too much for his own good. He was a good worker though. Provided well for the family and was a kind and thoughtful man. She looked at Ffion. For a woman in her mid fifties, she was still a good looker. Natural blonde hair, perhaps a few grey hairs, shapely figure (38G Cup for God's sake) and always well turned out, Pav had adored her. Maybe she looked severe to some people but Pav totally adored her. He had been in the Army, then the Police in Ulster. Linda had heard some of what had happened to him during those turbulent times. She admired soldiers who had served 'over there' as she called Northern Ireland. "The Forgotten War" was how Pav had described it. He hadn't forgotten though. His headaches served to remind him, if nothing else did. He once told her about his dreams, nightmares more like, and Linda had felt sympathy if not empathy for him. Linda knew as well, from Ffion, that Pav had nightmares about things that had happened in Ulster. Linda had even gone so far as to ask friends who were 'in the know' as it were, about Pav. She had met with a wall of silence and had even been told to keep out of things that did not concern her. On one occasion, when Ffion was flat out, drunk on the sofa, Linda had chatted to Pav in the kitchen of Ffion's house. He was sober but in a thoughtful mood. It turned out that, some thirty years before, Pav had lost a good friend in Belfast and blamed himself. That day was the anniversary of the event and Pav had been distant all evening. Ffion knew why Pav was distracted but, instead of being supportive, she had gotten herself blathered. Linda chose not to think about that at the moment. Her task was to look after her friend and see her alright. She leaned over and topped up the glasses. Wine was the friend they both loved.

"Do you remember the time he took your dog to the vet?" She said. "That woman who's dog wee'd on the floor, three times. Pav asked what breed it was and she said Pekinese. Then Pav said 'thank God it's not a Shitzu'!"

Both women laughed at the story, although it was harder for Ffion to find any humour in her current situation. For a while, they reminisced and found the good memories lightening the atmosphere. Ffion remembered telling Pav of an incident when she was only eighteen years old. She had gone to a nightclub with her sister. Ffion could not afford to be a slave to fashion and had worn a long woollen jumper over jeans and knee length boots. She had danced with a man who had groped her. When Ffion rejected his advances, the man had said "If it's not on offer, don't put it on display". Pav had said that if he had been there to hear that comment, he would have knocked the man spark out! So gallant was Pav. So protective of her. So, well to be honest, boring. Being loved was a wonderful feeling to Ffion but Pavs love was almost over powering. Still, beggars can't be choosers as they say. The two women talked some more about the events of the day. Ffion remembered when she, Damien, Pav and Andrew had gone to Northern Ireland for a week's holiday. Mainly it was so Damien could meet up with a girl he had met but Pav had wanted to lay a ghost to rest. They had stayed in a lovely guesthouse five miles from Lisburn where Pav had been stationed. On the second day they drove, in Pav's Mercedes, into Belfast and along the Falls Road. Pav had stopped in a side street and left the car without a word. He had stood on the corner, under a street lamp, smoking, seemingly deep in thought. Ffion had left the car and stood alongside him. She saw tears in his eyes and put her hand on his shoulder. As she did so, it was as if a dam had burst and tears flowed like mini rivers down Pavs cheeks. Damien merely sat in the car, looking at the scene and laughing. Actually laughing. Andrew went to get out of the car but Ffion told him to stay inside. After a few minutes, Pavs tears stopped and he wiped his face.

"I'm sorry" he said to Ffion, "I guess I needed that." Ffion asked why they were there and Pav had told her the story. Only about what had happened on that day though, not what happened after. Pav looked around and walked into the middle of the road. He turned a full circle, staring into the distance. For a moment, Pav looked as if he were in a silent rage, his eyes were wide open, his fists clenched as he stared. Eventually, he calmed down, as if something or someone had failed to accept his challenge. From that moment, for the rest of the holiday, Pav was a different person. He always seemed to be looking for something, or someone and being relieved not to find what he was looking for. Ffion had noticed things about Pav. When they went out, he never chose a seat with his back to a door or window. He always seemed to be scouring around, as if looking for potential threats. On one occasion, Pav had seen a little girl walk into the road, maybe two hundred yards ahead. Pav had shouted "STOP", causing the car drivers to brake and the mother of the child to grab her daughter. When the woman tried to thank him, Pav had walked off, ignoring her. Ffion told Linda about this and they wondered what had been going on in Pavs mind. Ffion knew about the friend he had lost but had never really appreciated just how much it had affected Pav, even now, all those years later. The next day, Ffion, Pav and Andrew set off to go to Londonderry to meet up with JK, an old comrade of Pavs. JK and Pav had served together for four years in Northern Ireland and had not met up for over thirty years. When they arrived, Pav left the car and was greeted alone by JK. Ffion was surprised at the warmth of the greeting. Pav and JK had hugged for ages before letting go. That seemed poignant to Pav and he smiled happily as he returned to the car. Pav had introduced them all to each other and they went into the house for lunch. A splendid lunch, provided by Kathleen, a lady, and one who gave justice to the word 'lady'. It seemed as if these two old soldiers had never been apart and the banter was rife. After lunch, JK and his wife, Kathleen, drove them around Londonderry and then over the border into Donegal where they admired the scenery. After a short ferry trip back to Ulster, they stopped at a restaurant for dinner. All in all, it was a pleasant relaxing day. And a surprising one for Ffion. Occasionally, a comfortable silence fell in the car, one that even Andrew did not disturb. Andrew was completely at home with JK and Kathleen and, if anything, Ffion felt left out. JK and Pav seemed to have a rapport that Ffion could not invade. There was obviously a past there but not one they would share willingly with her.

Three hours later, Ffion walked home, less drunk than she had a right to be. She glanced up into the sky and saw, for the first time in three years, *their* stars. That is what Pav had called a triangular group of bright stars. He had found out the official name for them once but she had long ago forgotten what it was. If Ffion was honest, she actually hadn't cared about the stars. Pav was the more romantic; Ffion was the more practical one. As she gazed skywards Ffion could only see seven in the triangle but knew there were more. Standing in her garden, one clear summer night, Pav had put his arm around Ffion's shoulder and pointed skywards.

"I think those are our stars," he whispered. "Don't ask me why but I do. Wherever I am in the world, I will look up at those stars and be close to you. When those stars die, so will my love for you." Pav kept his word.

The memory helped to clear Ffion's fuddled mind and guide her into a decision.

Walking into her modernly furnished living room, she saw her two sons and her daughter staring at her. Even the tv was turned off! Unusual in this house.

"What?" she snapped, looking at each in turn.

"What are you all doing here?" she slurred.

"Damien told us, about **him**" Amy, her daughter said. "You're not thinking of going to see him, surely? I mean, think about it Mum. You owe him nothing, absolutely nothing! He nearly ruined my wedding! Remember that!"

Ffion took a deep breath, "Yes, I do! **Don't** look at me like that. You never liked him, any of you. He loved me and I loved him but that wasn't good enough for you, was it? He was never good enough, was he? Come on, admit it! Not like your Father. Oh, yes, your precious Dad who slept with our friend, one who went skiing with us, year after year, yes, our friend who is half his age. And many others too! How the hell does Pav measure up to your Dad after that? Your Father was a *cheat*. End of. A cheat and he cheated on **me**. But I would still help him if he were in trouble." Their faces dropped, their mouths fell open. Amy shouted at her mother,

"Mum, he could be dangerous!"

Ffion responded in the same voice, "He's in a bloody coma! How the hell could he be dangerous?" She continued "Damien, I'll need your satnav tomorrow, and no, none of you are coming with me! This is something I have to do on my own. Now, I'm going to bed and **you** can all go home!"

No one moved.

"GO" Ffion shouted.

Amy started to respond "Hang on there Mum, it wasn't us who…"

"Don't go there! Just ***don't go there***! Just go home, ***please!***" Ffion shouted.

With that, she turned and fumbled her way up the stairs and collapsed, sobbing, on her king size bed that she and Pav had once shared, in love. "I'm coming, Pav" she whispered, "I'm coming." Suddenly, Ffion heard Pav singing in her head.

Think of all the things we've shared and seen, don't think about the things which might have been.

Ffion looked at the ceiling and thought that Pav had had a lovely singing voice, something he denied. 'Fancy hearing him sing that' she thought, 'straight out of Phantom of the Opera. Pav would often break into song, normally from Phantom. I wish I could hear him sing once more.'

*

I heard her voice. "I'm coming" she whispered. My heart lurched. Damn, if only I could move. My head screamed with pain but I paid it no attention. She's coming. To see me. At last! I felt like singing and so did. Think of all the things we've shared and seen…….

*

Chapter 6.

Next day, Ffion awoke at eight o'clock and lay looking around. She had no hangover, decades of over indulgence had conditioned her body to accept the abuse. Her head hurt but not too much. She turned on the television that Pav had bought and installed in her wardrobe and listened to the news. There was news on Northern Ireland and other hot spots around the world and Ffion found herself thinking of the times that she and Pav had lain on this very bed, watching tv. Even if Pav watched her more than the television. Ffion also remembered how Pav had pleasured her in the morning, many times. A voice in her head said,

I remember that too! EMS I called it. Early morning sex!

Ffion shrugged off the thought and returned to the task in hand. She then dressed, applied makeup and looked in the mirror. Pav would have said 'you look gorgeous, Princess' but she knew better. Often, Ffion would catch Pav looking at her.

"What?" she would ask.

"Just admiring the view," he would say with a happy smile on his face. She loved to hear him say that because she knew he meant it. Ffion was unaware that Pav was wondering just what was going on in her mind. What was she thinking? Did she love him? Ffion went downstairs and fed the dog and then went into the living room. Damien's satnav was nowhere to be seen and she fumed at the boy's attitude. The figurine had not been touched and she turned the key again. The music enveloped her mind and Ffion sat on the sofa, remembering, remembering. Something in her mind made her pick up the phone and dial a number she had not called in a long time. One call, to one person. When the call was answered, Ffion spoke quickly, not giving the other person time to reply. She was short and terse and, when she hung up, she hoped that this call would lay a ghost to rest.

It was nine pm in Sydney. Suzie sat looking at the half empty bottle of white wine that rested on the cushion beside her. Something else she had in common with Ffion. Suzie was Ffion's junior by some ten years but looked decidedly older. She had the same physical attributes but her face had been ravaged by time and she wore thick-framed spectacles. She also indulged in cannabis, something that Pav had found repugnant. He had never tried drugs and never would. It was all he could do to take aspirin. Another mellow evening. Suzie heard the old telephone in the kitchen jangling its annoying ring. She stood up unsteadily and answered the phone. She listened to what the caller had to say. Given that Suzie was thousands of miles away from Ffion, the line was crystal clear. And so was the message. When Ffion hung up, Suzie sat on her decking and gazed across at the Sydney Harbour Bridge, just a few hundred yards away. What Ffion had said was burning a hole in Suzie's heart. Pav dying. Ffion going to his side. Suzie ostracised by her older sister. Suzie was never to contact Ffion again; she had betrayed her in the most heinous way. Despite the glorious late evening sunshine that radiated around her, Suzie shivered and felt very very cold.

*

The house that Ffion lived in was hers and hers alone. When she divorced her ex husband, they sold their jointly owned house and she and Pav had moved in to a lovely three bed semi detached house that they had both liked. Not that Pav had much say in the choice. Ffion was buying it and Pav would just share it with her. Pav paid more than his fair share of the bills and decisions were normally joint ones. However, one sticking point was that Ffion would always remind Pav and Andrew that the house and most of its contents belonged to her. That made Pav feel like a lodger, one that was overpaying his keep. Amy took it upon herself to remind Pav that her mother owned the house and that, should anything happen to Ffion, then Pav would be out on the street. She also made clear that, even if Pav and her mother were living together, Amy was not going to lose her inheritance! Pav soon understood how Amy had risen to her current position of Sales Director. He wondered how many people she had stepped on to get there! Amy had once remarked, "I am always fully behind my colleagues"

Pav had responded in a whisper "All the better to stab them in the back!" Only Ffion's father heard Pav and he smiled despite himself. "You've got that girl worked out young man," he said. Pav smiled back, but the smile did not reach his eyes.

*

Twenty minutes later, Ffion threw her handbag and mobile phone onto the passenger seat of her old VW Golf and drove away from the house. She had dressed conservatively for the journey. Ffion knew that Pav loved to see her in jeans, knee length black leather boots and long woolly jumper and so she had chosen them carefully. She wondered if Pav would actually be able to see her. Her make up was just so and she knew she looked good. For her age anyway. Stopping at a shopping centre on the outskirts of Leicester, she bought her own satnav and asked the young assistant to set it up for her. She gave him the postcode of the hospital and listened to the basic instructions.

"Don't leave it in the car, love" the young man advised, "This model is very popular with thieves."

Ffion set off and headed for the motorway, listening to the monotone voice guiding her. She had bought Pav a top of the range satnav a few Christmases before they split up and he was so surprised. The voices on there were not as good as his impressions but he was, genuinely, surprised at the choice of present.

'I wonder if he still has it' she thought.

A voice in her head, Pavs voice she was sure, in his best Sean Connery voice, said 'don't hog the middle lane, you always do that'

I could see her, driving up the M1, sticking to the speed limit. "Don't hog the middle lane" I whispered in my mind, "You always do that". As if she had heard, Ffion moved back into the slow lane. I was shocked. Had she actually heard me? I felt in limbo, between life and death. But which did I prefer? The pain in my head is constant now. I can't exactly tell anyone can I?

'Pav's right' Ffion thought, 'I do hog the middle lane. Glad he can't hear me, admitting that he was right. I'd never hear the last of it'.

As Ffion settled into her driving, her mind wandered. Seven years ago, she and Pav had met at a charity fundraiser that he had organised. A young boy had Ducheynes Muscular Dystrophy and Pav wanted to raise money for him to go to America for pioneering treatment. The event was held in a restaurant north of where Pav lived and the hope was to raise several thousand pounds. In the end, it raised only a few hundred. It was a blind date, set up by Ffion's daughter in law who worked with Pav.

Pav had waited by the entrance, looking for someone who fit the description of the woman he as due to meet. Only one woman looked as if she was the person but she came into the room with a younger man, smiling happily. Pav thought that Ffion had not arrived and sat near the bar. Then, Anna said,

"Pav, this is Ffion, my mother in law".

Pav looked up and saw the woman he had noted earlier.

"But, but, aren't you with someone? He stammered.

"Oh no" the vision replied, "He just showed me the way into the restaurant."

Pav took a long while to look her over. Figure, 9/10. Makeup, 9/10, style, 10/10. In Pav's world, gorgeous! Ffion sat down and Pav got her a drink. He was driving so stuck to Cola but Ffion asked for vodka. Straight. They hit it off straight away and had agreed to go out for a drink one evening. Even though Pav had to ask Anna how to ask Ffion out for a date! He had seemed nervous and shy but Ffion knew from Anna that he was one hell of a Recruitment Manager and highly thought of in the transport Industry. She also knew that Pavs ex wife was giving him grief. She had left the marital home and taken her five-year-old son, Andrew with her. To make matters worse, she was denying contact and this was hurting Pav grievously. He had offered Ffion a lift home but she had declined, not wanting to seem too keen. Anna told her that Pav had gone back to his flat and firmly believed he had seen the last of this woman who had captivated him that night. It took Ffion two weeks to pluck up the courage to call and make the date. Then she had to cancel. Amy, having heard about her date, suddenly decided to take her out for a meal. Pav was great about it, philosophical and understanding. When they did meet, again, two weeks later, it was the most relaxing evening she had spent in two years, since her husband had deserted her for a younger woman. Two years of pain and tears and very heavy drinking. Two years of crying down the phone to her eldest son, seeking sympathy and retribution. Vodka was her tipple and she normally drank gallons of it. That evening however, she kept to two glasses of wine. Anna, Ffion's daughter-in-law, had told her that Pav rarely drank alcohol and so she was on her best behaviour. The bar they met in was in a posh hotel near where Pav had a flat. They sat and chatted, laughing uproariously at times all evening. It was only when they went to leave that they noticed the hotel was locked up and they had to rouse the caretaker to let them out. They laughed all the way to Pavs flat where they sat talking until gone five in the morning. The time passed so swiftly. By the time they parted, they knew all that was necessary and felt that life could be good, once again. They felt so comfortable in each other's company and agreed to meet again soon. It was to be sooner than they both realised!

When you left in a taxi to go home, my flat felt empty and lifeless. Wow, I thought, what a woman. Blonde, a few years younger than me but in much better condition. It was as if we had known each other all our lives. I felt guilty but I missed you. First date in two years but I was under no illusion, you won't be back. I dragged myself off to bed and managed a few hours sleep .The last thought I had before drifting into a light slumber was 'I must have liked you, I even paid for the taxi!' No work that day but I was on call and had to field many work calls. Recruitment. Sometimes I loved it, other times I hated it. Truck drivers can be a pain but, mostly, they are a great bunch. I found that sometimes a driver would call me just because he was bored and I did not mind. They worked hard for me and I felt obliged to be a sort of agony aunt if they needed one. It was round about 2pm when my mobile rang again. The voice at the other end was one I was not expecting.

"Three questions" you said. *"Are you at home, are you doing anything and can I come over?"*

"Er, yes, no and of course you can!" I replied, feeling very alive again.

Ffion explained "Damien is going to see City play and so I've got some free time. I'll see you in about 20 minutes if that's ok?" Yes it was. And so the adventure began.

Chapter 7.

After half an hour of driving, Ffion took the exit from the M1 and headed towards Stoke. She had been there only once before, with Pav and his son, Andrew. They went to a large swimming centre and had a great time, splashing, sliding and generally being silly. Considering that Pav could not swim, he had joined in with the fun and loved it as much as they all did. Pav drove, as Pav always did. He was an excellent driver, very experienced and calm.

You do not like driving on motorways if I recall, Ffion. Even dual carriageways can be a problem to you. The number of miles I must have driven you over the years. Not that I minded. It was a pleasure. Mostly. I remember the first time you took me to Whitby to meet your Mum and Dad. You were so nervous! Dad being an ex army Officer and me being an ex army lowly Corporal .They took my driving licence off me, you know. The one thing I could do in my life that no one could say they could do better. Even your Dad said I was the perfect driver and that was praise indeed! They were afraid I'd fall asleep or have a fit or something. That's when I knew just how serious the situation was .Not that it stopped me to be honest. What could they do if they caught me? Nothing. And I love driving, or should I say, I used to love driving. Over forty years without a blemish on my licence. Over a million miles driven in eleven countries but now that has all gone.

Ffion stared ahead at the dual carriageway. She had hated long journeys until she met Pav. He did all the driving. Even on that first trip home. She had told her parents about Pav and they had seemed happy for her. She was nervous about the meeting but in the end the weekend went well. They were even allowed to share a bed! Pav and Ffion's Dad got on famously and had many army things in common. Pav and John had known a lot of people from the same Corps of the British Army and reminisced all that evening and late into the night. As she went to bed, Ffion saw her Dad give her the thumbs up. Phew, what a relief. Was it too good to be true? When something seems too good to be true, it probably is.

That journey took just over four hours but it seemed like only seconds. I was nervous but not as bad as you. When your Mum said we should both stay in the flat attached to the house, I was amazed. And your Dad was a hoot. I never told you, Princess, but I knew him in Aldershot in the '70s. I was his driver for six months and, to be honest, hated him! He was an 'old school' officer. I was a mere driver, a peasant in his eyes. He doesn't remember me, thank goodness. When we discovered that we both knew Major Fear that was the highlight of the night. I regaled your Dad with the story of when the Major had knocked a horse spark out because it had thrown him. John could well believe the story and it was true. Honestly.

Ffion gave a start. 'Princess'. That's what Pav always called me, from day one. Now why did she suddenly remember that? Had she just heard Pavs voice in her head? She had felt flattered and embarrassed at the same time. Pav would call her Princess whenever he called her. That was only during the day though. He spent every night at her house. Initially, he had to creep in when Damien was asleep and be gone before the boy awoke in the morning. Pav never really understood why. Did he embarrass her, he asked? Her ex husband was a good-looking guy, whereas Pav wasn't. As Ffion had once joked, "I've tried good looking, now I've got Pav". No, she mused, it was because she was worried that Damien might react badly to her having a boyfriend. And, in Pav's defence, he tried his hardest to show Damien that he had his and Ffion's best interests at heart. Ffion remembered the look on Amy's face the first time he called her Princess in front of Amy! Her daughters eyebrows shot up and a sneering smile formed on her mouth. That was the first time she had introduced Pav to Amy, over dinner. Pav had been sleeping at Ffion's house for weeks by then but Amy was unaware. After the meal, Pav had collected the empty plates and cutlery and put them in the dishwasher. Amy had declared, "He's got his feet well under the table hasn't he?" Ffion had told Pav and he was not impressed.

"I was only doing what a good guest does, Princess" he had said. That night, Ffion felt a tension creeping in but chose to ignore it.

"They'll get to like each other" she believed.

I hated having to sneak around. Damien knew about me but not that we were sleeping together. We discussed it and decided that he ought to be told. When the time came, Damien was not surprised and showed no feelings either way. I always thought Damien was a sly, cunning child. I could see in his eyes that he thought my days were numbered with Ffion and that he would make sure of it. Oh yes, he made all the right sounds but his eyes told me the truth. I was an intruder. He had got his Mummy all to himself and I was not going to spoil that. Even his Dad said that he had felt like "the third person" in the marriage. Damien was always between his Mum and Dad and, eventually, his Father got fed up with it. So, I really had no chance of permanently getting my feet under the table.

"Check your fuel, Ffion, you're getting low".

Ffion suddenly looked at the fuel gauge. Almost on red. 'I'm glad I checked' she thought. A sign pointed to Services ahead and so she took the exit and filled the car up. She went to the café and stood smoking outside. Ffion felt calmer after last night's hysterics. Linda had given her advice. "Go and say goodbye", she said. "You'll never forgive yourself if you don't". As ever, Linda was right. Anyway, it was too late to turn back now. "I'm coming, Pav" she whispered, "I'm coming". But for the life of her, Ffion still did not know whether she loved him or hated him.

You're coming, Princess. Oh if only I could tell Ian. He's sitting here now, looking sad. Don't be sad my friend. I almost made 60. Anyway, any man who looks like Hal Cruttenden should never look sad! I have told Ian many times who he looks like, just not so camp. Ian is smiling now, almost as if he heard me.

Chapter 8.

Ian was looking at Pav. 'Such a waste' he thought. 'We had a few good times together, fighting fires, fixing roads, bbq's. I even didn't mind him saying I was a dead ringer for Hal Cruttenden. I bet Hal would be upset though.' Ian smiled. 'Yes, Pav, you could always put a smile on peoples faces. But you were always the first person you took the mickey out of.'

Ian was correct in his thought. Pav had never thought of himself as handsome. Quite the opposite in fact. His unusually shaped and sized nose and his jutting chin made Pav believe that he was ugly. Happily, not every woman thought that. Pav was once told that his personality would see him through life if nothing else did.

*

Ffion finished her cigarette and walked inside the services in search of a toilet. She felt strangely calm now that the shock had worn off. She was determined to see this through. It would be over soon and then she could move on with her life again. She might even ring.. well, maybe not! She glanced in the shop window and stopped in her tracks. There, on the bookshelf, were copies of a book, "The Missing Years", written by, of all people, Pav! Ffion held her breath and stared at the cover. There he was, back in his army days, crouching down by a landrover, deep in the heart of Belfast. His face bore a grimace and he appeared to be studying the camera. He

50

seemed to look straight into her eyes. Ffion grabbed her purse and, on impulse, bought a copy. She noticed that it was a signed copy too. Pav must have done a signing event here, at a motorway service station of all places! Outside the shop, she studied the look on Pavs face in the black and white photograph. There was a latent menace there, a look she had only seen once before. That was an occasion when her brother, Dicky, had said something to Pav about the army. Pav had stopped in his tracks, turned and, well, just glared at Dicky. Her brother had visibly shrivelled before everyone's eyes under the gaze. Instantly, the look was replaced by a smile and Pav had carried on walking into the garden, kids in tow as ever. Her nephew and grandson loved Pav. They had so much fun, reading or playing on the trampoline. Andrew joined in whenever he was staying and the four boys would be entertained for hours. Indeed, when her daughter came to collect Noah, he stated loudly that he wanted to stay with Pav! This, obviously, did not endear Pav to Amy. Pav dealt with the situation by picking up the boy and, laughing all the way, would place him in the car seat and promise even more fun next time. Very diplomatic. Now she realised why he had made such a good soldier. She glanced at a comment at the bottom of the front cover. A critic in London had written, 'A soldiers soldier, worshipped by his comrades, betrayed by his Government.' Now what the hell did that mean? Thrusting the book deep into her handbag, she ran into the toilet and threw up. This was getting too much. She had had no idea that Pav was an author let alone a published one. Although he had written a story called 'Jasper the naughty wasp' in just over an hour, one Saturday morning in her kitchen. Never 'their' kitchen, always 'hers'. A mercenary thought briefly entered her mind. 'He must have made some money, I wonder who benefits from his will?' She was shocked to receive an answer almost straight away!

Ah, yes, my will! What little I have goes to my son, Andrew. Who else would I leave it to? You? Damien? And Andy and Sharon will adopt Andrew.

'Why would he leave it to me? Ffion thought. After all, he has a son. *His SON!* Oh my God, what about Pavs son? The boy he fought so hard to get from the clutches of his evil Mother and her thug of a boyfriend. Where is he? Does he know? Ffion realised she was thinking aloud and scuttled into the café and bought a coffee. When she was seated, she grabbed her mobile and called Ian, hand shaking violently. He answered immediately.

"Andrew!" Ffion blurted, "Where is Andrew?"

"Are you coming to see Pav?" Ian asked calmly.

"Yes, I'm on the A50 near Derby but what about Andrew?"

"Andrew is on an extended holiday in Australia. Pav paid for him and Pavs friends, Andy and Sharon to escort him. We are trying to get hold of him but I doubt if he will make it home in time. Pav did not want Andrew to see him die so he sorted out the holiday. Sorry."

Ffion was puzzled. "Extended holiday? How long has he been there and how could a father send his son so far away when now is the time Pav needs him most?"

Ian sighed, "It was Pavs choice to make. Andrew would have gone through two months of upset whereas he is having fun right now. He went about three weeks ago and is not due back for another month. We've spoken to Sharon and it's up to her to decide whether or not to tell Andrew."

Ffion said, "I've just bought Pavs book, 'The Missing Years'"

"Yes, he did rather well with that book" Ian said. "We have a signed copy here. You should read it sometime, you get a mention. Chapter six I think. He wrote two more as well. The Missing Years explains a lot about Pav. So many things nobody knew about him. Getting published provided the money for Andrew to go to Australia, and a few other things too. See you when you get here."

The call ended, Ffion sat stunned by what she had heard. Andrew in Australia? Why Australia for goodness sake? Was that a dig at her? How could Pav do that? He and Andrew had such a close relationship, more like brothers really. Pav had cut the umbilical cord, held Andrew first and given him his first bottle. For four years, Pav had battled his ex wife because he just knew that she and her boyfriend were abusing Andrew. Eventually, Andrew came to live with Pav and Ffion but it was difficult for her. Ffion worked with children with Special Needs all day and it was difficult to come home to a boy who was the same. She tried though. Damien stopped being tolerant of Andrew and the strain on the relationship was immense. But sending Andrew thousands of miles away just so he didn't see his Dad suffer? It just did not make sense. To Ffion, what Pav had done was plain selfish, but then a memory tugged at her subconscious. Pav and Andrew talking on the decking one winters evening. Pav had said to his son, "Don't end up like me mate, please. Do better with your life, no matter what you decide to do. Where I failed, you should succeed. I will always support you. No matter what." He had then hugged his son and they sat in silence for a long time, tears streaming down Pavs cheeks. Now things started to make sense. As ever, Pav was protecting his son. Maybe Damian had been jealous of the closeness between Pav and Andrew?

I'm proud of my son. Not the brightest bulb on the tree but a heart of gold .He is so loyal to me and I know he will miss me terribly. I never told Andrew about my illness. He does not need that sort of heartache at just thirteen years of age. You can do that if you see him Ffion.

Chapter 9.

Ffion walked outside for another cigarette before continuing her strange journey. As she smoked, she looked at the back cover of the book. It described a war that was not a war, unless you were involved in it. She'd had a little idea about Pav's army life but not much. Even her father had said very little even though it was obvious he knew more than he was letting on. On getting back to her car, Ffion threw the book on the passenger seat and started the engine.

'Time to move' she thought.

The A50 was not very busy and Ffion was able to mooch along without having to concentrate too much. The new satnav helped, telling her about roundabouts ahead and which way to go. She let her mind wander.

'Let your mind wander, straight out of Phantom of the Opera' she remembered. 'What a weekend that was. Four Star hotel next to Lambeth Palace, home of the Archbishop of Canterbury, sightseeing all day then the performance in the evening. Pav had arranged for Champagne and roses to be in the hotel room on their arrival. The weather was perfect for a romantic weekend away and they had wandered along Millbank, through people celebrating ANZAC Day until, when they reached Old Scotland Yard in Whitehall, Pav had stopped. He looked down the side street, lost in thought or memories. Then suddenly he had said, "There's a pub round the corner, they are playing 'Streets of London', come on" Ffion had wondered how on earth he had heard that and, clutching his hand, had allowed herself to be led into the bar. Sure enough, that Ralph McTell was playing on the jukebox. Pav ordered two large glasses of house white wine and they settled into a booth and soaked up the atmosphere. Pav sang some of the words and Ffion listened to the emotion in his voice. She asked him why he had stopped at Old Scotland Yard and Pav had told her. Told her how, on the 8th March 1973, he had parked his army car outside the Central London Recruitment Depot and had left just two minutes before a bomb had gone off. He had touched her hand and said,

"If I had been there two minutes later, then I would not have met the most beautiful woman in the world, you".

That evening, they took a taxi to the theatre in London's West End. Ffion was resplendent in a low cut, black wraparound dress, and a red glass icicle shaped necklace glinting at her neck. Pav wore his best Jeff Banks suit, a black shirt and silver/grey tie. Entering the foyer, Pav flourished the tickets and they were shown to their seats. Pav had bought seats in the second row, right in the centre of the auditorium. Ffion glanced around, taking it all in.

"I'm so excited!" she told Pav. "Thank you for bringing me."

"No, thank you for being in my life" Pav responded, giving her a peck on the cheek. Pav felt proud as he sat with his love.

The performance of Phantom was everything Pav had said it would be, and more. Pav knew every word, every note and was enthralled, but then who in the audience wasn't? Pav had often told Ffion that he felt that he and the Phantom had things in common. Two ugly men who had fallen in love with beautiful women. Only for it all to go wrong. Two failed marriages were testimony to that. His comment was prophetic to say the least. From their seats in the centre of the stalls, two rows from the orchestra pit, when the chandelier came crashing down, Ffion could feel the downdraft. At the interval, Pav had pre ordered glasses of wine and he asked a fellow theatre goer to take a photo of them together, smiling at the camera, happy and so much in love. Such a romantic person, not like the men she was used to. A truly magic weekend. On the Sunday morning, during their wanders, they stopped in Southwark Cathedral and admired the architecture, in particular the stained glass windows in the Nave North Aisle, which depicted, among others, Geoffrey Chaucer and John Bunyan. It was here that Pav noticed a table, which held post-it notes with the invitation to write a prayer. Pav took out a pen, wrote his prayer and walked away. As they moved back towards the Nave, a young cleric approached Pav and asked if Pav had written the prayer that he held in his hand. Pav nodded and the cleric promised that it would be read out by the Bishop in the service the same day. The drive home seemed like a bit of a come down, Pav driving, Ffion re reading the programme from the previous night, often quoting to Pav from it. 'We were so in love, strolling, hand in hand like teenagers. Oh Pav, I wish we could start again!'

I wonder if you will' think of me fondly, when we've said goodbye?' It would have been even better if Damien hadn't called you every ten minutes! He did that when we went to 'Love Never Dies' as well. That was another great outing. Except you got jealous when I bought Natalie the bracelet as a thank you for organising the trip. What were you thinking?

'I was thinking that you fancied her for Gods sake! Yes, I know, I was wrong. I was insecure. You know fine well what my husband did, how he treated me by having so many affairs' Ffion shook her head. 'I'm talking to him as though he is here with me!' she thought. 'Damn him!'

'I am damned, Princess, that's for sure.'

*

Ffion and Pav moved in together on Boxing Day, only three months after meeting. Not one day or night in those months had been spent apart. All was idyllic. Storm clouds were hovering on the horizon, however. Damien didn't realise that Pav had actually moved in though. Pav kept his flat on for a while and Damien was told that the boxes of possessions were for a car boot sale. A neat deception by Ffion that should have sent a warning to Pav, that she was more than capable of lying to anyone.

Six months later and Ffion's daughter-in-law was holding a surprise anniversary party for her parents. Obviously Pav was invited with Ffion. At the event, Pav bought Andrew a high-energy drink because he was racing around with the other kids. Ffion went mad. She and Pav had a row and he and Andrew went home. In a way, Pav was old fashioned. He did not tell others how to bring up their children and did not expect to be told how to either.

I tried to explain to you why I bought Andrew that drink. He might have ADHD but it would have made very little difference to him except keep him from dehydrating. You kept telling me that Damien would not have been allowed one of those drinks, as if I had to do the same as you did. You never did understand, did you Princess? You never understood that Andrew was my son, not yours. You would not let me comment on how you brought up Damien, so why comment on how I looked after Andrew?

'I could never understand why Pav bought him that drink. He went so over the top when I mentioned it to him. I should have learned not to comment but never did.'

The atmosphere was thick with tension next morning. Damien said he was surprised Pav had not wrecked the house last night, a typical trouble making comment. Pav ignored him and he and Ffion had a heart to heart and all appeared to settle. Not for long though. Her parents were having a 50th anniversary party in York but Pav was not on the invite. Ffion said it was close family only but Pav was upset that he was not considered family at all. Her brother took his girlfriend, as did her son. Her daughter Amy took her boyfriend but only Pav and Ruth, Ffion's sister-in-law were left behind. Ruth was heavily pregnant so obviously could not travel the distance. Ffion called Pav several times over the weekend. Pav had vowed not to call her in case he was thought of as being possessive. At the same weekend, Anna and her boyfriend, Dave, announced their engagement. Pav felt low when he heard. Having worked with Anna for two years, they were firm friends. In fact, Pav had helped Anna get her promotion to another division of the company, on a much higher wage. Pav was proud of Anna and felt the distance between him and Ffion widening.

That hurt, Princess, and, if we are honest, it was the start of the rot. You could have asked your parents if I could travel with you but refused. Maybe I was just a cheap dog and house sitter? You just did not understand why I felt left out. I even got the opinion that you didn't want me there for some reason.

Ffion chose to ignore that thought. 'I'm losing it' she thought. 'Talking to myself, having imaginary conversations with him. Too much wine last night, that's all'. She checked the satnav again and felt reassured. 'Enough negativity' she thought, 'I'll never cope when I get there if I don't think nice thoughts'. Easier said than done though.

I never said our love was evergreen, or as unchanging as the sea Princess.

Pav lay motionless in the bed, mask over his mouth and nose, tubes from his veins to a machine and he could not communicate. He could hear still. Random thoughts came to his mind. 'How many men would pay to have a bed bath by a beautiful young nurse?' To lie in total peace and quiet, oh the freedom! But he wasn't free was he? Pav was trapped in a flesh and blood prison, no escape or time off for good behaviour. He had only one outlet and that was Ffion. Other thoughts invaded his subconscious, like the time Omar had told him "You are a dangerous man, Pavlos!" And all because, when the two of them had been having a drink in a bar in Polichrono, Pav had spotted three men, had correctly assessed them as criminals with evil on their minds, and he and Omar had dealt with them. All in a days work to Pav but to Omar, this man needed watching.

Pav found his thoughts wandering through his life. He saw a beautiful Serbian lady, Goriana and her daughters, Aleksander and Sofia, playing with Andrew on a beach in Greece. Two magical weeks with beautiful people, three females who revived in Pav a faith in the human race. He saw a gunman, on the balcony of a fourth floor flat in Belfast, aiming his Armalite rifle at soldiers. He heard the order to shoot, even though the gunman stood behind a woman who held a baby in her arms. Pav heard the shot and saw the man stagger back, the woman screaming. The gunman fell from sight but was not dead. He saw a Glasgow street fighter, a co-called comrade, coming at him in basic training in Aldershot, and then his vision turned to a military hospital, looking down at the body of his best friend. Although he was unaware of the fact, tears ran in solid rivers down his flushed cheeks and the monitors increased their noise. Pav cried, both inside and out, at the disasters of his life but cried most for the disaster that was Ffion

Chapter 10.

The A50 joining the M6 can be a tricky junction to cope with, especially for an inexperienced driver. Ffion started to flap when she saw the roads on the satnav and, instead of listening to the robotic voice, stopped in the inside lane. She stared wildly about her, like a rabbit caught in headlights. A voice spoke in her head,

Calm down, Princess. Follow the satnav, don't worry, you'll be ok. You can't sit there all day or you'll never get to me! Haha

Ffion put the car in gear and, very gingerly, followed the directions spoken to her. The voice in her head had sounded so much like Pav. 'Amazing what the imagination can do,' she thought. Rounding the sharp curve, Ffion found herself on the M6 and relaxed a little. A memory thrust itself forward in her mind, almost as if it was being forced into her conscious. Paris. By car, Pavs Gold Mercedes. Talk about springing it on her! Ffion's passport had expired and she had applied for a new one. Five days before the trip, which she knew nothing about, the passport had not arrived. She had wondered why Pav was more concerned than she was and left it to him to sort. The passport arrived on the Friday morning as they were leaving that same afternoon! She had had no idea where they were going, Pav had simply told her that he wanted to 'road test' his recently bought Mercedes. Pav was starting his own chauffer business and needed to see if the car was up to scratch. They had driven to Dover; Damien only called Ffion twelve times in those four hours, and took the Chunnel to Calais. They were searched thoroughly at customs, apparently because Pav was dressed in a tee shirt and jeans, not the normal attire for a man in a Gold Mercedes! From Calais to Paris and Ffion was pleased to see how well Pav coped with driving on the 'wrong' side of the road. She felt at ease but excited and refused to fall asleep during the long journey. In Paris, Ffion turned her mobile phone off, as did Pav. This was their weekend and they wanted no interruptions.

Their hotel was 4 star and looked it. Only a hundred meters from the Arc de Triomphe, the room was luxurious and so were the prices!

"Four Euro for one packet of crisps?" said Pav, "That's £2.80 a pack!"

They agreed not to touch the mini-bar either. Being as the time was past midnight when they arrived in Paris, they thought about going straight to bed but a sense of adventure gripped them. For the next three hours, Pav and Ffion strolled around the city, occasionally stopping for food or a drink, but not really heading in any particular direction. They absorbed the romantic atmosphere of the French city and felt at peace with the world.

Next day they did the usual tourist things, riverboat trip on the Seine, open top bus ride and then found a bar where they sat for hours, basking in the French sunshine. They watched the Parisian world go by, occasionally chatting to other British tourists but generally relaxing. Pav decided to get Ffion a souvenir and set off to buy a model Eiffel Tower. When a street seller tried to steal his wallet, Pav knocked him out and very nearly got arrested. Luckily, a Gendarme had been watching and all was smoothed over. Not by Ffion though. She was miffed and blamed Pav for spoiling their romantic break.

'Better if my wallet had been stolen and all my money gone, eh Ffion?'

'Better if you had stayed with me!' Ffion found herself snapping. 'For goodness sake! I'm talking to him again! What the hell is happening to me?'

Ffion's mobile rang. She glanced at the screen and saw it was Ian. Afraid to answer it as she was on the motorway, but also afraid she might miss something important, she put the call on loudspeaker.

"Hello"

"It's Ian, how far away are you?"

"Erm, the satnav says 130 miles, about two hours, if I push it. What's happened?"

She sounded worried, maybe not a bad thing, Ian thought to himself.

"No change" Ian replied, "But don't rush. He'll hang on, I'm sure of it. How are you feeling?"

"Tired. He's talking to me, in my head. I think. I'm not sure. I keep hearing Pav saying things, it's weird. We relive old times and he, well, he *talks* to me! I think he's in pain too. It's the way he seems to talk. Am I going mad?"

Ian paused. "Maybe you should take a break. Get a coffee and a cigarette. Don't fight it. If Pav is talking to you it means he has something to say. Something he needs you to know maybe? Or maybe you *are* imagining it, it could be your subconscious saying things you couldn't or wouldn't say to Pav? Anyway, relax, better to get here late than not at all eh?"

The line went dead.

'A Japanese General told me that, many moons ago. Corporal, he said, to get there in a hurry is important but to get there alive is imperative!'

'Yes, I remember you telling me about that, just one of your many anecdotes! You got a bit like the BBC, repeating yourself!'

'One repeat you never tired of was when I told you I love you. Or have you tired of it?'

"The last time you said it was when you told Linda that you loved me" Ffion replied. "Don't go there, I know what I did was wrong and she should not have called you. I thought you hated me for what I did."

'I did, for a few seconds. I was hurting. I was worried. Do you know what Linda said back to me? She said "I know you do. We all know." Damien said you had gone missing and told Linda that I had done something bad to you. That's why she rang me.'

"I didn't know he had said that, are you sure? Linda said nothing, just that Damien was concerned."

'I told you in my text, I heard Damien say it. Why don't you believe me? You always believed him and never me. Call Linda and ask her. At least she won't lie to you.'

'To be honest Pav, I really don't want to talk about the past.'

I'm losing my future Princess; don't deprive me of my past, please!

'I don't want to deprive you of our past, Pav. I just don't want to re live it just now.'

Pav bit back quickly, *Oh ok, shall we just wait a few weeks and then re-live it, Ffion?*

Ffion looked out of the side of the car. Flying almost alongside was a Kestrel. She remembered another kestrel, not too many years ago. After a moment, she relented.

'Do you remember the kestrel?' she thought to Pav.

Yes, I remember the kestrel. As if it were yesterday, Princess. December 2009. Although we are re-living the past. Are you sure you want to go there?

"Yes" Ffion came back. "Might as well."

You were in the kitchen, standing at the window washing up while I went for a cigarette on the decking .Quite often we would stand out there, sharing one cigarette. That day was a cold, crisp but very sunny day. One of the few that month. Snow lay delicately all around the garden. The rose I bought in honour of my mother was rock hard. The top of the fence panels held an inch or so of virginal snow. I was at peace with my life with you. I lit my cigarette but never got to smoke it.

Before I had taken a breath, a magnificent site unfolded before me. From the South flew a beautiful bird, a Kestrel, which landed on the fence panel, not six feet from me! I was stunned. I froze, not wishing to scare this beautiful creature away. The Kestrel sat a while before turning its head towards me. She looked me up and down, almost with disdain and then looked me squarely in the eye. Her piercing look made me feel so small .I believed that she was looking through me, into my inner soul. I found that I could not turn away. I literally could not move. I instantly nicknamed this bird Kes, if only in my mind. Kes and I continued eyeing each other for some 5 minutes, as long as it took my cigarette to burn away, slowly, ignored. When it reached the tip, I still held onto it, warmth soothing my otherwise cold fingertips .If I had been burned, I would not have cared. Our eyes were locked together until, seemingly tiring of my company; Kes stretched her incredible wings and flew away to the North. For what seemed like an age, I stood on your decking, (never ours) feeling lost, lonely, wondering where Kes would go to now. Who else would she grace with her presence? I actually felt a tinge of jealousy. When I came back into the house, you asked if I was alright as I seemed to have tears in my eyes. I told you it was just the cold outside but I had felt moved, touched by something I could not explain. I still can't explain what I was feeling that day.

'Yes' Ffion thought to him, 'I remember the look on your face as you stared at the bird. If you had won the lottery you couldn't have looked happier. You bored everyone with that story for weeks.'

Sorry if it was so boring to everyone! I just thought it better than talking about exhaust pipes or Manchester bloody United!

Ffion wanted to keep Pav talking. She asked a question,

"How was life in the wilds of North Wales for you both?"

Pav chuckled, 'I'm surprised you want to know to be honest. The summers were great, plenty to do. Mind you, during the first winter we had plenty to occupy us as well. When the snow hit, we were isolated most of the time. Nine foot drifts along the lane leading to the farm. Andrew had great fun though. Sledging etc. We would also walk into the village and dig people's cars out of the snow and then walk the five miles into Caernarfon. He loved that and, when we got there, we would have a drink in the Castle Arms. Just the one, maybe a hot chocolate or coffee. Then we'd walk back home, again helping people. We had the lambs to feed too. Andrew was so good at that, so tender and caring. Maybe he'll make a farmer one day! Then, the second winter was wet and very windy. A couple of times we went without electricity, as did many places, but we missed out on the flooding, thank goodness. Andrew was resilient all the way through and we made it into an adventure. He never went without. Not once. He was very happy. He often talked about you. I tried to protect Andrew you know that. From the weather, from his mother, from pain. I can't protect him from this though, can I?

*

Ffion could not answer that comment. She suddenly thought about a course she had attended at the school where she was a teacher. She had learned that, generally, a person in a coma has very little brain activity. It would seem that, what little activity was going on in Pavs' brain, was being used to try to communicate with her. She wondered if he was able to breath unaided and how his blood pressure was coping. Pav had often had high blood pressure but it was put down to the stress of his job and wasn't dangerously high anyway. Ffion remembered the advice given by the course instructor, how to react if you ever have to visit someone in a coma. Tell them who you are, talk to them normally, show love and support and maybe even play them their favourite music. It had all seemed useless information at the time. After all, when was she ever going to be visiting someone in hospital who was in a coma? Especially if that someone was talking to you through your thoughts. And, she shuddered at the thought, if that someone was a person who had loved you with all their heart, body and soul.

More services loomed ahead and so Ffion decided to take Ian's' advice and have a break. She took the satnav off the windscreen and placed it on the floor out of sight. It was mid afternoon now and she wondered where the time had gone. For some reason, Pav had been silent these past few minutes. 'Sleeping probably' she thought. 'Or dead already. He must be tired, mentally if not physically.'

Pav remained silent. His thoughts had been lacking cohesion but he knew that was part of the problem. Pav knew that, if he thought too much, then the pain would be unbearable. He had come to terms with the fact that he could communicate with Ffion through thought and had tried to speak to Ian as well. That avenue was closed however. He did not try to talk to Andrew, that would have freaked his son out. Pav focused his attention on Ffion.

Ffion sat in her car for a few minutes. Yesterday, she had few cares in the world. The normal week ahead, making sure Damien went to work, housework, maybe a trip to town shopping. Now? Well, now she was on an epic journey by her standards. Two hundred miles to see a man die. Not just any man, a man who had loved her with a passion she didn't know was possible. What killed that passion? Many, many things. Pav's behaviour towards her family, her behaviour towards Pav and his son, the fact that Pav could read her like a book, the knowledge that he was right in so many things but she could not admit it, not even to herself. The way he could not, or would not, get on with her daughter. One incident had killed her feelings of love for Pav though and she refused to think of it right now. She felt tired and leaned back in her seat. Five minutes rest maybe. Just five minutes. Her eyes closed and she drifted into a deep and dreamless sleep.

Chapter 11.

She woke an hour later with a start, feeling cold. Something had disturbed her. She looked around, all seemed normal. What was it then?

'It was me Princess. You were sleeping, oh, and snoring!'

'I do not snore!' Ffion thought, stemming a smile despite herself. 'You always told me I did but I don't.' She heard a chuckle.

'Yes you do! How many times have I listened to you when you were asleep? One of the most beautiful sounds in my world, I promise. Or at least, you did. I don't know about the last few years do I?'

Can I ask you something? Pav continued, *why are you coming to see me, Ffion? I am dying, a hopeless case, so why would you travel so far, just for me, a man you hate?*

'Why?' Ffion replied, 'because that's what I do. I have no reason other than it's what I feel I should be doing'

And yet no one wants you to, do they?

'Ok, lets play this your way.' Ffion said, out loud. 'Let's assume you really can talk to me and hear me too. Answer this, how is my Father?'

Do you really want to go there? Your choice Princess.

"Yes, tell me oh great one! If you can of course"

'Your Father died three months ago Princess .Heart attack. You thought about telling me but decided not to. Don't worry; I wouldn't have attended the funeral. I sent a wreath though. That way, no scene was caused was it? I was sorry though. I could have seen you again. Nice speech by your brother to be honest. He and Nino were well looked after in the will, just like you said they would be. Girls always came a poor second in your Dad's eyes, didn't they?"

'You bastard!' Ffion shouted. "I wanted to tell you but, if you are so good, tell me who told me not to! Go on!'

'At least you admit that not telling me was not solely your decision. Who else, Amy told you not to contact me. Damien agreed and the only person who disagreed was Ruth. Am I right?'

Ffion calmed down. He *was* right. Maybe she *was* actually talking to him. Although he could easily have guessed. Still feeling like this was an out of body experience, she thought,

'Sorry, you are right. I'm so sorry. That must have hurt. So many things we did hurt you. I'm sorry.' Tears welled in her eyes and she grabbed a tissue.

Then she remembered what he had just said.

"Wait a minute. You said you sent a wreath, is that true?"

Of course it is, why would I lie? Are you saying it didn't arrive? If I were going to live I'd ask for my bloody money back! Fifty quid, wasted!

69

Silence fell noisily in the car. Ffion saw in her mind, her father's funeral. All the family and so many friends milling around, waiting to go in to the concrete and glass crematorium, the sun putting in an appearance for the occasion. Everyone dressed in black, even Damien had a suit on, except his trousers were hanging off his arse. Before the ceremony had started, she had caught a glimpse of Damien with something that looked like a bunch of flowers in his hand, walking across to a rubbish bin. He had thrust the flowers into the bin and then, unbelievably, spat on them. She had been too upset at the loss of her father to mention it at the time, or too scared to find out the truth, but now. Now she knew what had happened. Minutes passed with neither of she nor Pav speaking.

Pav saw the images in Ffion's mind and was shocked. When he saw Damien bin the flowers he was not surprised but when he saw how Damien spat on them he was angry.

Nice. Pav thought. *Although to be honest I am not surprised.*

He spoke, quietly, almost apologetically.

You said 'we' just then. Does that mean that you finally accept that, maybe I was right? That your kids really did not like me? Or is binning my flowers a sign of endearment.

"Yes, I guess I knew all along but they are my children at the end of the day, and I love them, just like you love Andrew." she said.

You are trying to justify Damien's actions aren't you? Put it down to the fact that he only started to hate me after I had left. But you know that's not right, don't you? You know that's how he always felt. From the moment I came into your life .I am not being horrible here Ffion but may I just say, he was such a sneaky little shit? Try to hide it as much as you like but we both know the truth. Don't we? Think about the window in the kitchen Princess. I know he broke it and so do you. The glass was not just in the kitchen but on the carpet in the hall and the stairs. You went to his room and he was faking sleep. I was a cop, Princess, and a good one too. I can even see him do it now, in my void. That's what I call my present condition. Now, you can see it too. The ball, bouncing off the kitchen table, smacking the double-glazing? Watch as it shatters and watch his reaction! Listen to him coming up with the lies! Damien lied to you, so many times .You were such a fool! But then, you are his Mum. Even when we caught him smoking at thirteen, he tried to lie to me. You didn't tell his dad, you asked me to deal with it. At the time, I felt honoured but soon realised that his Dad would have gone mental and you could not let that happen could you? He could have said you were an unfit mother. Remember being pissed in Evington? Remember the phone box? The one you smashed when your husband refused to come and collect you? No, I am not seeing things Ffion, I was there! However, Damien could do no wrong but Andrew could do no right .Have I assessed the situation correctly?

'That was before we met, for Gods sake!' she snapped. 'How did you know about it?'

Pav smiled in his mind,

Like I said, Ffion, I was there. I was waiting for a hire car I was going to take to London. You were so pissed; even though it was only eight pm. Don't believe me? You had jeans on, black boots, a white blouse with a long woollen jacket, cream I think.

Ffion changed tactic, mainly to avoid answering the questions. She knew that Pav had summed up things correctly and had no intention of agreeing with him. Or his voice anyway.

'When did you find out about my Dad and how?'

'I found out just after you told Linda. You ran to her house and told her. You had two bottles of wine with you .Chardonnay. Just in case eh? When you went home, she called me. You need proof that I am really talking to you. Call her, now. Please.'

Ffion was stunned. She grabbed her mobile and called Linda. Linda told her that she had called Pav and apologised for interfering.

'But who told you?' she asked Ffion.

"Pav did" Ffion replied. "I'll tell you all about it when I come home, but you won't believe me!"

Linda put the phone down. Pav told her? She thought. 'What the hell is going on?'

*

Chapter 12.

Ian sat looking at the prone figure lying on the bed in front of him. He saw the tears coursing down his cheeks, saw the twitching of the muscles in his eyes and rang for a nurse. A doctor ran into the room and bent to look at the patient.

"Unusual" he said. "Tears may mean he's thinking. It's a good sign that he might regain consciousness, that's all though. However, if he's thinking sad thoughts then that could easily hasten his demise. If he does come round, he is going to be in terrible pain, physical and mental. I'm sorry." Ian sat back in the comfortable leather chair and sighed. He steepled his fingers under his chin and thought his thoughts. Ian thought about how Andrew would take the death of his Father. What would become of the boy? Pav had earned enough money from the sales of his books to ensure that Andrew wanted for nothing for a good few years. Pav had put money in trust for his son, over half a million pounds, so that Andrew could live in comfort. Pav had also ensured that Andrew would have a job on leaving school and that Andrews mother saw nothing of the money. Given that Pav had earned a nice living from writing, he drove a twelve year old 4 x 4, had an ageing sports car and a modest house. Ian remembered the lottery win too. One million pounds on Pavs first ticket had come his way but it was the second ticket that had seemed strange to Ian. One hundred thousand pounds was on the winning ticket. On the same week that Pav had won the jackpot. When Ian asked Pav about the other ticket, he had simply said, "I found a good home for it".

'I can hear the doctor now. He thinks I may come round for a short while. That's all though and probably not for long. I'll wait for you.'

Ffion left her car and stood outside smoking. Her mind was blank, afraid to think in case Pav heard her thoughts. People walked past, paying her no attention. As she stubbed her cigarette out, her mobile rang. It was Damien. She sighed, 'he must be home from work now and worrying about his dinner' she thought. No chuckle from Pav this time.

"Hello" she answered.

"Where are you?" Damien almost demanded. In his Leicester accent, it sounded like "Where are yor?"

This was tiring and she did not need it right now.

"On my way to Wales, with a new satnav that I had to buy this morning. Thanks for that Damien, really bloody helpful!"

"'S not my fault, I told you not to go. I dunno why you're bothering!"

Ffion terminated the call and put the phone on silent.

'Not now Damien' she thought, 'not now'.

'You're not saying anything, Pav. Why?' she thought.

'I told you from day one Princess, I did not want to come between you and your family. I told you there would be friction and I always tried to keep out of things but when you live with someone you love, it's not easy. My just being with you came between you and your children. I tried, believe me I tried. How many times did I tell you that I felt like an intruder when Amy came round to see you? She paid a passing interest in Andrew but made a point of ignoring me. That hurt Princess. I was supposed to be your partner, not a visitor to your life. I know I said too many things that I shouldn't have but I won't apologise. I could have said so much more. Even your sister told you that.'

Ffion stopped herself from replying out loud. Not in a public place, not here. People would think her crazy. Maybe she was?

Five minutes later, restocked with cigarettes and chewing gum, Ffion started the car and rejoined the motorway. Her mobile phone buzzed but she ignored it. It was Damien again. He called a further five times before giving up. 'Probably can't find the pot noodles', she thought. She heaved a sigh of relief when the phone fell silent. For the rest of the journey, Ffion would only answer the phone if it was Ian. Or maybe Linda. Or, God forbid, Pav!

The traffic was heavier now and she had to concentrate on the female satnav voice that kept her company.

Ffion decided to start a conversation. Anything to keep her mind off her son phoning.

'Tommo was asking the other day, if I would make that casserole you made. You know, the beef one that went down so well?'

'Casserole? Bloody casserole?' Pav stormed. 'Did he mean the Beef Stifado I made that took three and a half hours? Casserole indeed. Even then, you tried to tell me how to make it. You'd never cooked a Greek dish in your life but you decided that I was doing it wrong!'

'Pardon me for speaking!' Ffion responded, indignantly. 'I'm sorry they didn't know the *exact* name for it. Just be glad they enjoyed it. And I was only trying to help and what did you do? Snapped at me and then Dicky for standing up for me!'

*'Ah yes, Tricky Dicky. How is the expert on **all** things? I mean, who needs Google when there's a member of the Stone family around, eh? Your brother who earns £80k per year but still borrows, interest free, from his parents' Pav chuckled. 'Still calling his twelve year old son darling and sweetheart? No wonder he got bullied at school.'*

'You can be such an asshole, can't you?' Ffion retorted. 'At least he's not in a hospital, dying!'.

No sooner had she thought it, she regretted it. Just like so many things in their relationship. Pav was silent for what seemed like ages, maybe waiting for her to continue. She didn't.

Pav took the initiative after a few minutes.

'Well Ffion, what the hell do I say to that? Glad to see you are reverting to form.'

*

Chapter 13.

Guilt racked Ffion and she sat staring at the road ahead. Just over an hour before she reached the hospital where Pav was, actually and really, dying. His life was ending whereas she could go home and return to normal. She had been feeling unwell these past few weeks and had gone to her own doctor for tests. The results had not come through yet, that would be a good sign, she thought. She thought about turning the car round and going home. Maybe Damien was right, maybe it was a waste of time. But then she realised that Pav would still talk to her and so she wouldn't be free of him just yet. Anyway, curiosity got the better of her. Would Andrew make it in time to see his Father before the end? Was Pav waiting for him too, or just for her? In a fit of frustration, Ffion checked the mirror and moved into the outside lane. Flooring the accelerator, she flew past other cars, the speedo inching up to 100 mph. She had never, ever, driven that fast and she was scaring herself, let alone other road users. Gradually she slowed the car back down to 70.

'What are you trying to do? Kill yourself?' Pav asked.

His voice had concern in it and, yet again, Ffion felt guilty.

'I don't know, maybe.' She answered. 'Would that make you happy?'

No reply. Silence, apart from the thrumming of her tyres, eating up the miles to Wales. Even the satnav was quiet.

When the reply came, it made her jump.

'I think you know the answer to that. But just in case, no it would not make me happy. Anyway, I'd get the blame from your family, I always did. Always the blame, never the credit.'

*

Chapter 14.

Christmas 2010. Pav had risen at seven am and spent nearly six hours preparing and cooking the Christmas dinner for Ffion and all of her family. Twelve people around the sumptuously dressed table, all reds, gold and silver decorations, pulling crackers, telling jokes, and enjoying the lavish meal. How so few people could possibly eat all of the Turkey, Beef, Ham, all the trimmings, and wine by the bucket load and desserts Pav had no idea but they would give it a good try! And then the previously unthinkable happened. Amy took to her feet, thanked her Mother for such a wonderful spread and proposed a toast. To her Mother, a magnificent cook. When it was *Pav* who had done it all. Pav had looked across at Ffion; she looked back, and said nothing, absolutely nothing, merely smiled. Pav had raised his glass in mock salute to her and left the table. He walked onto the decking and lit a cigarette. Ruth, Ffion's sister-in-law, joined him and placed her hand on his shoulder. Nothing was said, there was no need. She understood but even she did not dare speak out. Pav spent over an hour on the decking, just thinking. Eventually, Ffion came out and sat near, but not next to him. Neither spoke. After only a few minutes, Ffion stood and went back into the house, to join her doting family. She had not spoken one word to Pav. She hadn't even looked in his direction, just smoked a cigarette and left him sitting there. Pav was devastated. He felt more alone on that Christmas day than he had ever felt in his life. Even during those 'missing years'. That Christmas day was the worst Pav had ever experienced. He felt unloved, unappreciated, and totally invisible. He would rather have been shot at on the streets of Belfast than go back into the house, however, as he lived there, he had no choice. Ffion never explained why she had not said anything. Not even, 'well, Pav did help!' The smile on Amy's face spoke a million words. She had got her message across. 'You might live with my Mother but I will never, ever, accept you.' Maybe that was the day that Pav gave in, tired of fighting to prove himself. Nothing he did made any difference so he might as well give up trying. Pav had wanted to die that day. Pav could see and re-live that day in his mind, unaware that Ffion saw it also.

Ffion watched in the video of her mind and saw how Pav had felt. At the time, she felt that he had overreacted to what Amy had said but now? Other occasions came into her mind, times when Pav had seemed to sulk about something or other. Now, it all made sense.

"Did you really want to die that Christmas Day?" she asked.

*'I still do, Princess. I **want** to die. Not alone though. Can you understand that?'*

'Yes, I understand. Can you hang on long enough?'

'I hope so. I do forgive you, you know. It doesn't matter now that you could not acknowledge me that Christmas day .It mattered at the time though. I was starting to realise that you were falling out of love with me and that, no matter what I did, I could not stop you.'

Time to change tack, Ffion realised. This could develop into an argument and that would be pointless.

'So, what have you been doing these past few years?' she asked.

'Apart from dying, slowly and painfully, do you mean? Pav asked, bitterly. *I'm sorry, ignore that. If you mean has there been anyone else then no. I had found who I was looking for and then lost you .We moved to North Wales, I got a driving job and wrote a little. Had a few stories and articles published and then wrote a book. I sent it off and, somehow, they liked it. I became an author and, much to my surprise, got published. Three times. Then I was lucky enough to win the lottery. I saw couples, maybe our age, walking hand in hand, so in love and that hurt. Was I jealous? Maybe. You never had that problem though did you? I even stopped going out in case I saw people in love. One day, I was in the local pub when a woman who was a dead ringer for you walked in. I dropped my pint on the floor. Then she looked straight at me and I realised it wasn't you. I wasn't even drunk. It knocked me for six and I stayed out of town for weeks. Even after winning the lottery, I stayed home, not knowing what to do. It was Andrew who persuaded me to go out and spend some of it. Strange how my life has turned out. Never had much money but, now I've got plenty, I'm going to die. Before I can make the most of it. I see you've got "The Missing Years" on the seat next to you. Don't read it until I'm gone, please?'*

'Ian said I get a mention, Chapter 6 he thinks. What are the other two books called?'

'Forgotten Victim' and "A Humbling of Heroes".

Ffion checked the book. Neither of the other two was mentioned, maybe she was talking to him after all. It all seemed so unreal, so stupid!

'Do I get a mention in those, too?'

I'm sorry but no. A Humbling of Heroes is about those people who made a silent contribution to peace in Northern Ireland. Forgotten Victim is a novel. You would find it boring I suspect.'

'I should have realised you would get a book published. You were always good with words.'

Yes, you said that many, many times Ffion. Mostly when I had caught you out lying to me.

Again, Ffion chose to ignore the barbed comment.

'No love stories then? Ffion asked, amusement in her voice.

No, my imagination is not that good!

"Ouch! I asked for that one didn't I?

Pav said nothing. Ffion listened to the satnav telling her to take the next exit and keep left. She left the M6 and joined the A55 heading west towards North Wales. Darkness was fast approaching and she wanted to arrive before nightfall. Ffion was nervous driving in the dark; especially now she needed driving glasses. She brushed away a strand of long blonde hair and glanced in the driving mirror. She was shocked at what she saw. Bags under her eyes, which were red with stress, lines furrowing deeply across her forehead, and lips with no makeup. She glanced at her hands and was shocked to see they looked like skeletons.

'I look a mess' she thought.

'No, you look beautiful. To me anyway.' Pav thought back.

'You're the only one who thought so.' She replied.

'Really? Think about that comment and tell me again.'

Ffion knew straight away who Pav meant and spoke without thinking.

'I used him for sex! Damn you, he was a mistake!'

'One you kept making though. One you kept telling me about too. Of course, that was just to hurt me wasn't it?'

"Like you said Damien was not his fathers son?" Ffion snapped back.

Ffion, one of the many things you hated about me was that I saw things for how they are, not how people say. You know why I said what I said. You also know I was right, don't you? There is one advantage of my condition at the moment, Princess. Being midway between life and death gives me a certain, 'insight'. I am able to see things that you and I did. I know the truth to so many situations now. Trust me, Ffion. I know! I know why you were so hard on Andrew but soft on Damien.

'I was not!' Ffion retorted.

Look into your mind Princess, Look at how Andrew would always have to do things that your own son didn't. Look at how Andrew would be told to wash his hands after going to the toilet whereas Damien was ignored when he failed to do so. There are so many things that I saw but you didn't or couldn't. I am not the only person who said you were too soft on your son but hard on mine. I know why too. You realised that you treated Damien like gold dust. For some reason, Damien is your little precious, no criticism of him allowed. All your family realise that Ffion. You could not change and so you decided Andrew should be differently treated. I know other things too, Ffion. Would you like me to show you Amy disposing of the crystal picture of Andrew and Noah? Twenty-five pounds of my money, thrown into her rubbish bin. And you knew about it.

Ffion changed the subject, more out of embarrassment than anything else.

'Tell me then, how did you end up where you are? I mean, how did you know about the tumour?'

'Ah, a long story Princess. It all started with a holiday. We had sleeping bags but no tent.

Ffion interjected then.

"What about the six man tent we used in Kent?

All the guy ropes had been cut Ffion. It was not useable. I have no idea by whom or why. Anyway, Andrew wanted to go camping so I bought all the gear, hiking sticks, wet weather gear, back pack etc and off we set. We arrived in North Wales on the Saturday of your birthday. I just could not bear to be so near to you and yet so far. Andrew and I went up Snowdon on the train twice and he asked if we could walk up it. As we had the equipment, and, as the last time he and I attempted the walk it had ended badly, I agreed. I was so impressed! Being as Andrew would normally moan about walking thirty feet to the car, when he made it to the top of Snowdon, and thoroughly enjoyed every step, I was full of admiration. Even you would have been impressed.

"That's not fair Pav" Ffion responded.

Maybe so but he did so well. About five hundred feet from the top, I was knackered and told him I might not make it. He took my pack from me and led me to the summit. Then, the weather closed in and Andrew said it was not safe for me to walk down and he booked us on the train back to Llanberis .He showed such maturity that day. It was then that I realised that Wales was the perfect place for him, and therefore, for me. We discussed the move and both agreed. Eight weeks later, we were here .It was tough for a while, new place and so on but we adapted. I never forgot you though.

How could I? I rented a house on a farm and Andrew was so good with the animals. He even helped the farmer and made a sick bay for poorly lambs. We would get up in the middle of the night and feed the orphan lambs and they grew to love us .One lamb in particular would follow us around the farm like a puppy. All the campers would come to us for help and advice. We love it here. Sorry, let me re phrase that, I used to love it here. Now? Well that's a different story. Then, when the headaches got too bad, I finally decided to get medical help. I sometimes wish I hadn't. I never told Andrew when I was ill. I just sort of hid away, ran from it. I never ran from anything in my life until then.

Ffion could imagine the scene and felt a strange mix of happiness, sadness and jealousy. Pav continued,

Remember that time in Leicester that Andrew phoned you because I was in such agony with the headache? Remember telling people that it was alcohol related? Well, I am happy to say that you were wrong. No, please don't try to justify your comments. The brain scan at that time showed that I had a bruise on my brain, nothing to worry about, they told me. Been there years they said. Ever since I was in Northern Ireland. Too much blunt trauma to the head causing the brain to swell. It will go down, they said. Trouble is, that bruise hid the tumour and it was only when I insisted on another scan, just a couple of months ago, that the real reason was discovered. When I was being sick, literally, everyone thought it was alcohol related. It wasn't though. I thought it was the tablets they gave me to ease the pain. Vomiting was part of the symptoms. The constant ringing in my ears was difficult to get used to though. So was losing my balance, something you and Damien found hilarious. You said I was putting it on or had been drinking. Alcohol consumption is, for me at least, a thing of the past. Oh I still have a drink, on special occasions but nowhere near the amount we used to get through. I didn't tell anyone, not even Andrew. I couldn't. I was a coward in that I didn't want sympathy and also I didn't want anyone to tell you. I hoped to die quickly and quietly. Well, quick is guaranteed, quiet, maybe not. I wanted you to find out when my executor contacted you. Will you think of me fondly, when we've said goodbye?'

'Yes' Ffion said quickly. 'Yes, I will. Despite what I said once, we did have some good times. How has life been since we, erm, parted? I mean, it must have been difficult with Andrew. What about his mother, did she ever contact him?

Yes, she took me to court for contact. Then never turned up for the hearing. Said she was on holiday in Devon and forgot! Andrew didn't want contact and told social workers so. The court told her, in not so many words, to stop causing trouble and go away. He hasn't seen his Mother since he was taken away from her. He never had Christmas presents or birthday presents. Nothing. As for anyone else in my life, no. There could have been one but my heart just wasn't in it.

Ffion decided to take the bull by the horns and ask Pav about something that had hurt her deeply, something that had sealed their fate. She had never been one to tackle issues head on and had dealt with the betrayal of her sister and her partner in her own way.

'Pav, I never thanked you properly for my 50th birthday party. You even flew Suzie over from Australia. Dad told me how much that cost, over £1000! Why did you do that? I know you were always kind and thoughtful but that seems a bit extreme.'

'She's your sister, the rest of the family were to be there and it seemed a shame to leave her out. Anyway, I suppose I liked her. A brash Aussie voice but a heart of gold. Even if she expected everyone to do everything for her.

Pav thought for a moment before continuing.

Princess, there's something you need to know.

'Here it comes' she thought, 'the confession at last.'

Do you remember the night before Suzie announced she had Herpes? You and I had another argument in the garden and you stormed off to bed. Suzie pulled me into the living room and kissed me. Really kissed me. She was wearing your Paisley print dressing gown and she put my hands on her breasts and kissed me again. I was stunned. I had no idea how to react. I simply walked out of the room and upstairs. Before I came to bed, I brushed my teeth and scrubbed my hands until they were raw. I am ashamed to say I could have been tempted. Physically that is. But in my heart, I knew I could never have sex with your sister. That would have been the ultimate betrayal. You and I had just had an argument, she had taken my side instead of yours, and Tricky Dicky was looking smug, almost as if he were glad that we'd argued. You said next day that I was distant with her. That's why, Princess. We never talked about what nearly happened but I never looked at her in the same way again. And then for her to announce she had a sexually transmitted disease really got me thinking. Why, if she even thought *she had herpes, did she offer herself to me? I can only think of one reason. That she wanted to give it to me, and then to you. That way, you would have known that she and I had had sex. It's almost as if she were trying to get revenge on you for something that had happened in the past. Maybe she was jealous that you had found happiness? Maybe I'm wrong and if so I am, truly, very sorry. I paid for Suzie to fly over from Sydney for your surprise birthday party because I believed that would make you happy. That's all.*

Chapter 15.

Ffion heard the truth in Pavs' voice. Her mind felt numb. Any doubts that she was actually talking to him were now dispelled. What he had just said was not all new to her but she believed him, totally. She had had her doubts but things slotted together like an emotional jigsaw. Ffion had known that something had happened that night but not exactly what. Suzie had laughed at her when she confronted her the next day but there was a sly look in her eyes that Ffion recognised. Suzie had not even denied the accusation. Then, twelve months later, Pav had paid so much money to fly Suzie to England that she firmly believed they had had sex that night. That was when her love for Pav died and she vowed to get him out of her life, one way or another. It never occurred to Ffion to actually ask Pav what, if anything, had happened that night. She believed that he would lie and that would make matters worse. Like Pav so often said, she adopted a pacifist attitude. Ffion took her time getting Pav out of her life. To her shame, she made life very difficult for both him and his son. Why, she had even accused Andrew of stealing the Love Never Dies bracelet that Pav had bought for her. Even when Pav bought her another and she had also found the original, Ffion had continued with her vendetta. When she was introduced to her new lover, Ffion had no qualms about having sex with him and letting Pav find out. Damn it, at that time she was enjoying getting her revenge and having sex at the same time. But it was all wrong. So very wrong. She was afraid to answer straight away. 'Deep breaths' she thought. Her sister had urged her to behave like a slapper. A fifty four year old slapper at that. And she had done so. At least with one man and Pav had found out about it and was hurt. She had slept with Pav three times in one week and the 'other' man twice that same week. And then she had told Pav. At the time she had been pleased with the expression on his face, now, she was ashamed.

'I am so sorry Pav' she said. 'I honestly believed that you and she, that you had,' She could not bring herself to say it.

No Ffion, I could never have betrayed you in that way. I am many things but not that. I may have liked her but I never fancied her. I truly loved you, you and only you. I never realised that that is why we parted, why you seemed so hell bent on destroying our relationship. At least I can die in the knowledge that it wasn't just me who wrecked all that we had.

'Oh my God what have I done?' Ffion pulled off the motorway and into a lay-by and cried, and cried, and cried. She sobbed and screamed such was her pain and guilt.

'I can't do this anymore!' she sobbed, 'I have to go home.'

Don't you want to see me die Princess? To see that I am gone from your life forever? To say your goodbyes to the man you believed had actually slept with your sister? Do you now believe that it never happened?

Ffion did not answer straight away.

Pav stayed silent. He let her anguish subside before speaking again, the sound of his voice hollow at the back of her mind.

'It's in the past now Princess. Don't let it eat you up.''

Ffion waited until she felt calmer before replying.

'Yes, I believe you. I am so sorry and, no, I don't want to see you die but you are going to and I am going to be there for you. I failed you and Andrew but not now. Can you ever forgive me?'

Pav said nothing. Hesitantly, Ffion pulled back onto the motorway and, a few minutes later a police car pulled alongside, the occupants giving her quizzical looks. She smiled and they pulled ahead.

'Thanks' she said to Pav. 'You're my Guardian Angel today. Actually, I think you always have been.'

I'll never be an Angel, Princess, not after the life I've led. My direction of travel is surely down, not up when I shuffle off this mortal coil.' He chuckled and sang two lines from Love Never Dies, 'Once upon another time, I knew how our story would end.' You and I growing old together, Saga holidays, matching Zimmer frames, telling people just how much in love we still were. As usual, I was wrong wasn't I? So much for my being perceptive, eh?

Ffion confessed. 'Now I know you are telling me the truth. You always said you were perceptive and I thought you would know why I fell out of love with you. If you had slept with her, you would have known but, if nothing happened between you and Suzie, you would not have known, would you? It's so bloody obvious, now. Nothing happened and I ruined our relationship. I am so, so sorry Pav. Can you ever forgive me?'

There was no answer. She tried again many times but Pav was not talking. Or maybe he was unable to talk. At that moment, the pain in Pavs head was unbearable. He put it down to more than the tumour, that it was actually the realisation that he had yet again been victimised for something he had not actually done. Ffion carried on towards North Wales, eyeing the Snowdonia Mountains in the distance, rising majestically towards the sky that would soon be greeting Pav.

A thought arose in her mind.

'That call you had, the one offering you work in Turkey. Tell me again, why did you turn it down?

Pav took a few minutes to reply.

It was driving supplies in to Iraq from Turkey. Yes, thirty grand for three months, which I might not have returned from. Dangerous work but who cared? I always loved danger, maybe that's why I fell in love with you? You and Andrew would have had a few quid to get by but, at the end of the day, not enough. To be honest Princess, I wanted to end my days with you and Andrew. Earning a lot of cash in such a short time was tempting but you and he were my main priorities. Thinking back now, I would have rather died in action than in a hospital bed, like the old fool I am. I believed once that I was invincible. I had my army training and a family of thousands of other soldiers so what could harm me? Now I realise that the one thing that could really bring me to my knees is love. Why did Suzie do that? Did she hate one of us?

Ffion had no answer to that question. Suzie was back in Sydney now but one day she would come over to England and then Ffion would get the answers. Too late for Pav though. She tried talking to Pav again but he did not respond. His mind was taking a journey back over thirty years. To when he was really invincible, when he knew his life might be in danger but nothing could hurt him. Even after the riot in Belfast that left him critically injured in a Military Hospital, he still believed he was untouchable. As he lay in bed, attached to machines by tubes, breathing his last into a mask, Pav relived some of his happier army days. If his face had allowed him, Pav would have smiled. All he could manage though were a few blinks of the eye. He had reacted to some of the reaction tests and the medical opinion was that he was not yet in a PVS, a Persistent Vegetative State. Pav showed some very slight reactions, which may have been good but, given the state of the tumour, was not altogether helpful.

"If only things could have been different" Ffion whispered, more in the hope that Pav could not hear her words.

Oh they could have been so different, Ffion. You see, I've been given an insight into how my life would have turned out if I had changed two very important decisions in my life.

"Go on" Ffion replied, "What were the decisions and how would life have been very different?" She knew she sounded sceptical but still needed to hear what Pav had to say.

Shortly after 4pm, Ffion pulled into the hospital car park and parked as near to the entrance as she could. It had been a long and emotional journey. Just as she entered the large imposing building, her mobile rang. This time, she answered it. Damien.

"Yes" she snapped.

"Where are you Mum?" her son asked. "We're worried about you."

"I'm past the point of no return, Damien," she replied. "Don't call again." Ffion turned her phone onto silent. Taking a deep breath, she walked into the Reception and asked for Pavs room. She was directed to a private room on the Intensive Care floor. Ffion walked with a steady purpose, trying to get Pav to answer her thoughts, but to no avail. She felt saddened. Had what she said upset him beyond all reason? She felt that, if she could be there next to him and apologise, maybe he would talk to her, one last time. As she approached the room, a well-built and smartly dressed man came through the door and smiled at her.

"Ffion, I presume?" Ian said. "I'd recognise you anywhere, just from the photo Pav has on his phone." Ian showed it to her. It was a picture taken in France of the two of them outside a Parisian café, Pav raising his glass of lager in toast to the photographer. Ffion sobbed.

"How is he?" she asked Ian.

"Not good I'm afraid. About an hour ago he took a turn for the worst. His head moved from side to side and he cried out. He was shaking uncontrollably and tears fell from his eyes and he seemed totally distraught."

"I think I know why" Ffion explained, "We've been talking to each other. I told him something that would have devastated him."

Ian raised his eyebrows, "So you were right then? Did you manage to make peace, put things right between you?"

"I don't know. I sure as hell learned a lot though. I put my trust in the wrong people and now it's too late. He hasn't spoken to me for the last hour. I think I'd like to go in now, please, can you give us some space?"

Ian took Ffion to one side and said, in a hushed tone,

"Before you go in, you need to know that Pav will have changed since you last saw him. Prepare yourself."

Ian hesitated before opening the door for her.

*

Ffion hesitated then walked into the room. She stared at the figure on the bed. Pale, almost grey, so thin his skin seemed to hang off his skeleton, eyes closed and hands almost like claws, his right hand in a tightly clenched fist, as if ready to punch someone, or something.

She called out "No, this is a mistake! That's not Pav, it can't be! He was so, so,..." She was lost for words. The Pav she knew was not fat but slim, brown greying hair and a permanent smile on his face. This, corpse, lying in front of her just could not be him! Pav looked more like eighty years old, not the sixty he nearly was. So skinny, pale skin looking shrivelled, eyes closed and hands folded across his chest as if he were dead already. The grey stubble on his chin made Pav look more like a down and out than the man she had fallen in love with. His hair had gone almost white and Ffion was glad she had not seen him deteriorate over time. Selfishly, she realised that she could not have coped with that. All Pav needed now were coins on his eyelids. Ffion wondered briefly what Amy would have said had she seen him now. Ffion looked at Ian hopefully. Ian spoke softly.

"Full of life? It's him I'm afraid. He started dying, physically anyway, about five years ago. Before you and he split up. He started dying mentally the day he moved out of your house. Two months or so ago, he just gave up living. Knowing that he was about to die, gave Pav a sort of kick up the backside. On the day he found out, he made all sorts of plans so that everybody would be well looked after. Even you, Ffion. He survived for as long as his son had need of him. Andrew is with friends now. He will be well looked after. I met Andy and Sharon. They adore Andrew and, well, Pav left a lot of money for Andrews's welfare. Andrew needs his Dad no longer. You don't need or want Pav. Pav only had one need, one desire but even that was denied him, wasn't it? One night, Pav had a few drinks. Rare for him these days. We sat by a fire in the campsite and he told me all. I mean *all*. I never thought I would see him cry. Real tears, tears of pain, not just physical but mental pain. Did you know he saved a girls life in Belfast? He bought her a ticket to London so that she did not have to live in the ghetto she had been born in. Did you know that he would have given his life for you or any of your family? He would too. Do you know just how much he cared for your Grandson, Noah? Do you realise what it did to him to be told he was not allowed to see that wee lad again, just because of arguments you and he had? Because your *precious* daughter had it in for him? She used her son as a weapon as much as his ex wife used Andrew. He beat her but did not have the energy to fight Amy. You didn't know that he had written three books, or that he mentioned you in one of them. Why didn't your family tell you about them? The publishers even sent you a copy of each but I bet Damien got rid of them. Damien must have censored your mail, just like he read your texts, because Pav wrote to you, only a few weeks ago, telling you things. I've known Pav for only two years, you knew him for seven. And yet, you didn't really know him at all, did you?"

Chapter 16.

The door closed softly behind her and she sat beside the bed. Pav was lying on his back, wired up to monitors and drips. His breathing was steady now but the salty tracks of tears still showed on his leathery, ancient cheeks. Ffion felt her own eyes watering. Here was the man she had once loved, a man who had loved her more than she could ever deserve. A man she had once believed had betrayed her whereas it was she who had betrayed him. A dying man with whom she had to make peace. Acting on impulse, she took her mobile phone and took a photo of Pav in his present state. She then sent it to her daughter, Amy, with a message.

"I hope you are happy now. He soon will be."

She then turned her phone to silent. No way was she going to try to justify her actions. Ffion reached over and took Pavs hand.

"I know you can hear me Pav, it's me, Ffion. I would tell you about my journey but you know it already." she said softly. "I want to say how sorry I am. If I could turn back the clock I would do. I told you once that, if we did not have our children, our lives would have been perfect. I meant it. Not in a nasty way. I have wronged you in a terrible way. I can't ask you to forgive me because I can't forgive myself, or Suzie. If only you could talk to me, just one more time."

She remembered her training and spoke softly but positively.

"I do love you, you know that, don't you?"

No response and so she carried on "I remember how nice you were to Aunty Joy. She adored you and I felt a little jealous though God knows why! She was eighty years old for goodness sake! You always said she was a real lady and I think you would have done anything for her. Richard noticed that she thought the world of you. Why didn't I appreciate you more? That poem you wrote when she died was so lovely, touching, honest! Oh Pav, give me a sign that you can hear! Please, I beg of you!" Her tears stung her eyes and cheeks as they fell to her chin; past the skin cancer scars that lined her lips.

Ffion remembered suddenly a motorway near Bristol. She and Pav had driven down to see Damien play football for his school. It was a cup final and their team had lost. On the way home, Pav was in the left lane when he saw the car in front pull out to overtake a truck. Then the truck pulled out too. The first car swerved, hit another car and hit the central reservation, spinning several times before coming to a standstill facing the wrong way in the fast lane. By this time, Pav had pulled onto the hard shoulder with his hazard lights flashing. Without thinking, he grabbed his hi-vis coat and jumped out of the car. He believed that someone in the crashed car could be injured and so he raced across three lines of traffic, waving at the other drivers to stop. Only one did, a coach driver who slewed across the three lanes, effectively blocking all traffic. Pav checked that both drivers were ok and then called the emergency services. He made it clear, no injuries, no fire, damage only collision. Ten minutes later, an ambulance arrived, followed by two fire engines. Pav got angry at the emergency control and pointed out the waste of money and resources. It got worse. Shortly after, an air ambulance hovered overhead and Pav used the land ambulances radio to tell them they were wasting their time. Eventually, a police officer arrived. As he got out of his patrol car, Pav had actually clapped! Pav and Ffion had been there an hour before they could continue their journey home. Ffion had called Damien on his mobile to warn the coach driver that the motorway was closed and that there would be delays. When they got going again, Pav calmed down. Ffion wondered what she would have done today, if something similar had occurred. She had admired Pav for taking control of the situation and also for putting the safety of the other drivers before his. Then she got angry because he could have been killed. Pav reassured her that he knew what he was doing. Damien put it more bluntly.

'Always playing the bloody hero' was his mature assessment. Ffion knew though that Pav cared about others more than himself. He was not being a hero, just helping.

Ffion looked down at Pav. She had never seen a dead person before but she knew that Pav had seen plenty. Starting at age eleven when he saw his own father dead from a heart attack. Then, in the army, he had seen people shot and others blown up. He had seen death in car crashes too. It had only got to him once. When he saw a six-week-old boy who had died of a cot death. Pav had been mortified and took a long time to get over it. He was even invited to attend the funeral, even though it was at a cemetery in Belfast where Pav could have been killed. Obviously he went, typical Pav. No thought for his own safety. The parents guaranteed that Pav would not be harmed and had told the local IRA that this was one 'Brit' who could be trusted. As Pav was called in Greece, 'the little man with the big heart.' Now, he was looking death full in the face. He had seemed so calm about dying when he had 'spoken' to Ffion. Was he being brave or did he just not care? Ffion decided on the latter although she knew that very little frightened Pav. He was not religious as far as she remembered, although he did attend church at Easter and Christmas. And he always put a crib on display on Christmas Eve.

'So' she thought to Pav, 'what happens now?'

Slowly, very slowly, Pavs hand moved. It rose to her face and the cold fingers stroked her cheek, gently, like silk on skin. Ffion closed her eyes and felt rather than saw his tenderness. The fingers moved to her lips and traced their outline. Ffion kissed the fingertips as tears flowed again. Her thoughts went to the better times of their relationship. She saw that there were many, not few as she had told Pav. Her heart ached to have this man with her again, happy and healthy.

The back of Pavs hand caressed her neck and before she realised it, his fingers clamped themselves on her throat. Such was the power of the grip that Ffion was unable to breath. She thought at first she was dreaming but, when she tried to remove this vice like hand, she could not. Desperately she tried again and again then she tried to grab the alarm button. Her mind swam and panic rose in her mind. For the first time in her life, Ffion was truly frightened.

'Please Pav' she thought, 'Please don't!'

* * * *

Chapter 17.

I can hear Ffion talking to me. At that moment I hate her but I also love her! My mind is in turmoil, a battle of emotions raging inside. One cannot win. Do I take her with me? Do I let her stay? *Does she deserve to live or die?* I have to die but she doesn't. *Not yet. Not now.* She destroyed our relationship! *She didn't know the truth!* Kill her you fool! *Let her live, you are not a murderer!* She turned you into a murderer!

Pav awoke for just a split second and shouted,

"She did not make me into a murderer, I did that for myself!"

Pavs brain fought with his emotions, only one could win. The tumour seemed to tighten its grip on the brain, forcing rationality away. Almost ten years of pent up anger and frustration burst forth, giving superhuman strength to a dying man.

Ffion could hear the battle for reason raging in Pavs mind and she could see the toll it was taking, written on Pavs face. She felt a tinge of hope; surely he could not do this? Ffion grabbed Pavs hand and squeezed. At the same time, she begged for her life. She croaked out "Let love win, Pav, not hate."

"Hate? Ffion I have hated you for a few seconds but I loved you for always!"

Ffion looks at Pav, confusion showing in her eyes.

"I know you loved me and I destroyed that love. I am so, so sorry!"

Reason takes over again. I am not alone but soon I will be .I feel a presence, a shadow of the past looming over me. I cannot take her with me, now is not the time for her. God will be my judge. Forgive me.

A second later, Ffion felt the grip ease and the hand went slack. She gasped for breath, massaged her throat and gazed at Pav. His eyes were open now but no life showed in them. The monitors screamed their banshee like sound but the medical response came too late. The door burst open and Ian and the Consultant ran in. Doctor MacPhee saw Pav, leaning to one side, hand draped over the side of the bed, as if pointing to Ffion. The doctor ran to that side of the bed. Ian saw that Ffion was crying and gasping for breath and mistakenly thought that she was upset. He failed to notice the red finger marks on her throat. Ffion placed her hand up to cover them. She would never tell of what had happened. She felt she owed Pav that much.

Ian saw that Pavs right hand had opened and the piece of paper it held was lying on the blanket. Hesitantly, he picked it up and read it aloud.

'Dearest Ffion, you had some tests done at the doctors recently. You don't know the results yet. I do. We all die Ffion, some sooner than others. I came into some money last year. Below are the details of a bank account I set up for you. The money will pay for private health care. I love you Princess.'

Ffion listened to Ian read the letter again. She could not believe what she had just heard and experienced. Her mind returned to what had just happened. Ffion was shocked. Pav could, and most probably should, have killed her. But, at the last moment, he had relented. Why? Ffion asked the question in her mind. The answer, when it came, was straight from Pav. His voice filled the room, even Ian heard him say,

You have to ask why Ffion? Because I love you Princess. And, as the great man wrote, Love Never Dies! Goodbye, Princess.

Now this is not the end, it is not even the beginning of the end,

But it is, perhaps, the end of the beginning.

Epilogue

Pav was cremated six days later at a crematorium in North Wales. His ashes were scattered at the peak of Mount Snowdon, as Pav had requested. A special train to the summit had been hired for the event. Smoke belched from the engine as it wound it's way along the rack and pinion track that had been laid so many years before. The journey up was sombre; Pavs ashes were in a silver urn on the footplate of the engine. At last, Pav had gotten to ride in a steam engine. This was a journey that Pav and Andrew had taken many times but this would be Pavs last. The view from the top was spectacular and Andrew had cast his father's remains to the winds, tears rolling down his cheeks. No clouds spoiled the view and the sun shone down on the mourners. Pav would have appreciated the day.

Ffion stayed in Wales for Pavs funeral. She wore, for the occasion, her black wraparound dress and the red icicle shape necklace. The music Pav had chosen to accompany him into the hereafter was Celine Dion singing 'Just Walk Away' and Sarah Brightmans' version of 'Time to say goodbye'. As the coffin slid silently on greased casters into the gloom behind a black velvet curtain, the theme from Harry's Game played softly. The congregation shed many tears. None more so than when Ffion read an extract from a poem by John Keats: -

"I almost wish we were butterflies and lived but three summer days, three such days with you I could fill with more delight than fifty common years could ever contain."

Ffion imagined Pav looking down at her as she read. Most of the congregation were surprised at the sad smile that crept across her lips. Finally, she blew a kiss at Pavs coffin and returned to her seat.

It was Andrew's turn to read a poem he had written for his father.

Dad,

I may not always have been happy

But I wasn't always sad,

I may not always have been a good boy

But I wasn't always bad,

I know you did your best for me

You did the best you could,

I'd bring you back from Heaven

If only I could.

I'm going to miss your laughter

I'm going to miss your smile,

I promise to stop crying

If only for a while.

I don't know why you left me

Why you had to go away

But Dad, there's really something

I really want to say,

I love you Dad

I love you,

And I know you love me too,

Rest well my lovely Daddy

With love, from me to you.

Andrew sat down next to Ian and sobbed quietly. The congregation was silent for a few minutes before the service continued. The vicar spoke about Pav as if he had known him all his life, but in fact the two had never met. Ian presented his script to him twenty minutes before the service.

Andrew had shown an exceptional braveness at the funeral of the father who had loved him so strongly. He would then go to live with Andy and Sharon, back in the East Midlands, well provided for and well loved. Ian and Andrea said their farewells to Pav at the foot of the mountain, in the station restaurant, hugged Andrew fondly and went home to their house on the farm.

At nighttime, Andrew would lay in his bed, reading his fathers books, the ones he had signed especially for his son. He would shed many a tear but would also remember all the good times they had shared. During the funeral, he refused to even acknowledge Ffion.

Whilst waiting for Pavs funeral, Ffion read 'The Missing Years'. What she discovered sent her mind reeling. After Pavs send off, Ffion drove home to the East Midlands and summoned all of her family to her home. She also invited her two closest friends, Bev and Linda. When everyone was seated, Ffion made an announcement. She stated that, from that day forth, Pavs name was never again to be mentioned in her presence. She stated the reason as 'you could never talk about him with respect when he was alive, I doubt if you can now he's dead'. She also told them about Pavs bequest and the reason for it. Amy jumped up and tried to hug her mother but was pushed away. Ffion shed no tears for her own predicament, but instead placed a large photo of her and Pav on the solid oak bookcase, next to the music box. It was the one of them in Paris, Ffion smiling and Pav raising his glass of beer in salute to the photographer. Ffion sent her family away and sat in her living room, listening to the music box and crying softly. Damien kept well out of the way. Wisely. The next day, Ffion instructed Damian to move out of her house and in with his father. She needed time to grieve and could not do it with a belligerent, lazy teenager around.

Ffion died on Christmas Day; exactly six months to the day that Pav had breathed his last. She had cirrhosis of the liver, caused by alcoholic excess. From the moment Pav passed away, to the moment she died though, Ffion never took another drop of alcohol. She had been hoping for a transplant but died before one became available. She never spoke to her sister again.

When Ffion was taken into hospital for the final time, she insisted on taking with her two of her most prized possessions, a photo and the music box. These were to be buried with her. At her deathbed in hospital were her two sons and her daughter. They wept and held her hands as she spoke her final words.

"Think of me fondly, Pav, think of me fondly."

This is…The End.

Or.... Is it?

The woman stood to one side throughout the proceedings, neither a part of them, nor apart from them.

The woman was Allegra, only one person there would have known her, Andrew. She had taken care not to be seen by him however.

Allegra and Pav had a past, one she had not forgotten. She owed this man who had died in such agony a huge debt.

She had loved him, as no other woman had loved him, nor ever could.

Pav had saved her life and she had saved his. Would anyone ever know the truth?

Allegra kept her sunglasses on, her straw hat covering her face, as she grieved, wept, and mourned the man she knew.

As the parties split up at the bottom of the mountain, Allegra moved to the side of the railway track, on the platform at Llanberis Station, and wept, openly, totally drained of feeling for anyone or anything else. Tourists watched her, staff at the station shop watched her, but no-one moved towards her.

Eventually, Allegra picked up her tan coloured handbag, dabbed her eyes and walked off, to where, nobody ever knew.

As she walked, she remembered, Pav, Carmel, and many others.

She whispered to the wind, in the hope that it would carry to Pav, wherever he was now,

'I loved you Pav, I so loved you. I miss you and one day, we will be together again. Thank you dear Pav, for everything. God speed 'old son', God speed"

Then, she was gone.

This is a work of fiction. Names, characters, situations and places are the products of the author's imagination or are used fictitiously. Any resemblance to actual events or persons, living or dead, is entirely coincidental. Any medical inaccuracies are mine.

This book has been an emotional roller coaster for me.

I have used names of people because I like them, not because they relate to any real people.

I had one true love and lost her. That is my biggest regret.

I would like to thank Ian for being my sounding board, a good friend, my proofreader and advisor. I thank Andrea for giving constructive criticism and for being absolutely right!

I thank Lord Lloyd-Webber for creating 'Phantom of the Opera' and 'Love Never Dies', two shows of pure genius. And for his permission to use extracts from these shows in my book. His genius gave me inspiration and comfort when times were tough.

I thank my son, Daniel Jack, for his patience, his fortitude and his testimony that my book was, "okay, I suppose". Praise indeed!

I also thank the women who have graced my life. One in particular. She knows who she is, for she was, *my* Princess.

Thank you for reading "When we've said goodbye". Think of me fondly.

Printed in Great Britain
by Amazon